Between Here and Knitwear

CHRISSIE GITTINS

**UNTHANK
BOOKS**

First published in Great Britain in 2015
by Unthank Books of Norwich and London

A CIP catalogue record for this book is available from the British Library

ISBN 978 1 910061 25 1

Unthank Books
PO Box 3506
Norwich
NR7 7QP

www.unthankbooks.com

Contents

By the same author:

Poetry for Adults
A Path of Rice
Pilot
Armature
I'll Dress One Night as You
Professor Heger's Daughter

Poetry for Children
The Listening Station
Now You See Me, Now You...
I Don't Want an Avocado for an Uncle
The Humpback's Wail
Stars in Jars

Short Stories
Family Connections

Radio Plays
Poles Apart
Starved for Love
Life Assurance
Dinner in the Iguanodon

As Editor
Somebody Said That Word
Thoughts in Corners

For my dear family and friends;
and in memory of my mother and father,
and David and Mabyn.

1 Curlew

On my first day at Heap Bridge Primary School I was the only one who didn't cry. We used wide notebooks with soft blue covers; there were three faint lines on each page for writing and a huge space for drawing. Next to the blackboard was a wooden chair with a thick twisted rope wound around its back. If a child was naughty he or she would be tied to the chair. Barry Smith was often tied to the chair.

On the rippled ridge at the bottom of the blackboard balanced a cardboard box of coloured chalks. At playtime my friends and I took the cherry red, the cornflower blue and the primrose yellow chalks and drew huge tiered birthday cakes – dripping turreted castles lit with a host of burning candles. We filled the board as high as we could reach then rubbed them out and started all over again.

In the second year we moved up to the next classroom along the corridor. The bell went for the afternoon and Mrs Kershaw appeared at the door. We all ran for our desks.

"Good afternoon, children."

"Good afternoon, Mrs Kershaw."

Mrs Kershaw was tall and wore pencil skirts and fitted jackets. She always renewed her lipstick for the afternoon so her mouth was crimson and glossy; it stood out from the rest of her face.

"This afternoon, children, we're going to start growing our peas. Who has remembered to bring in a jam jar?" Everybody's hand went up apart from Barry Smith's. "Barry, I have a spare one you can borrow. In just a minute I'm going to give you all a piece of blotting paper and a dried pea. I soaked the peas last night to give them a head start." She held up a pea between her finger and thumb. "I want you to roll up the blotting paper and slot it into the jam jar like this." The rolled up blotting paper sprang out inside the jar making a lining. "Then I want you to push your pea between the glass and the blotting paper."

We all rolled and slotted and slid our pea down the side of the jar.

"We must remember to water them. The blotting paper mustn't dry out," said Mrs. Kershaw. "And I'm going to give you a sticker for you to write your names on."

Every other day we queued up at the white Butler sink in the cloakroom to gently drip water onto our blotting paper; then Mrs Kershaw stood the jam jars in a line along the window ledge to catch the sunlight.

Each morning when I arrived at school I went to check my jam jar. A shoot was growing upwards towards the sky. After two weeks the shoot shot out of the top of the jar. It was one of the longest on the ledge. Barry Smith's had hardly grown at all.

On Friday Mrs Kershaw said, "We must all water our peas before the weekend. Line up at the door. And how are we going to wait in the cloakroom?" We all put our fingers on our lips. She took down each jam jar and carefully placed them in our waiting hands. The forty of us stood patiently in line. I ran my spare hand along the rows of pegs and drawstring shoe bags. I was near the back of the queue. Barry Smith was behind me and Cheryl Chadwick was in front. When Cheryl finally got to the sink she held her jam jar under the dripping tap and dribbled water onto the blotting paper; it changed from light to dark blue. Barry Smith pushed me. I pushed Cheryl. Cheryl dropped her jar. It bounced once then smashed. The pieces of glass ricocheted against the side of the sink. The shoot snapped off her pea and wedged itself in the plughole.

Mrs Kershaw bustled up to the sink.

"What's happened here?"

"She pushed me," said Cheryl, pointing her finger at me. Mrs Kershaw gave me a steely look.

"Did you?"

"Yes, but…"

She didn't let me finish.

"Well then you can give your pea to Cheryl."

Barry and Cheryl's jam jars remained on the ledge. Barry had written his name in red wax crayon. His letters slid down the label. Cheryl's pencil name was neat and crisp. Day by day their shoots grew taller. Tendrils curled beside the lime green leaves.

Barry lived not far from me. We lived at the end of a terrace on Bury Old Road and he lived on the estate behind. Our Accrington red brick house had real leaded windows. Mum said you could tell they were real leaded windows because the diamond panes would catch the sunlight at different angles. The paintwork was yellow and there was a red peony in the garden which always had a mound of tea-leaves underneath where Mum had emptied the pot.

One afternoon when I was walking home from school I could hear footsteps behind me. I turned round – it was Barry Smith. He started chasing me. I ran past the electricity generating station and turned the corner up the hill. Barry overtook me on the bend. Ahead were two men and a woman walking alongside each other, blocking the pavement. Barry saw his chance. He stood beside them so that to get by I had to run into the road. I ran around him. I could hear the screeching of car brakes. A green Ford Popular stopped inches from my coat. The leather seats folded forwards and the driver and passengers lunged towards the windscreen. I could see the driver's round spectacles tipped sideways on his face. He shook his finger at me. I stood, locked to the spot, with my hand over my mouth. As they drove on the three elderly lady passengers stared at me and shook their heads.

By now Barry was a running dot on the horizon. I walked further up the hill, past my house and climbed over the stile onto the fields. The fields rose into Bluebell Hill then stretched down the valley to factories exhaling smoke and steam, and then to the string of houses where Mrs Kershaw lived. In the far distance was the spur of Holcombe Hill with its sturdy black square tower. Along the fence by the path, sheep's wool hung at intervals, snagged on the barbed wire. Mum's favourite grass glittered in the wind; she called it 'silver spoons'.

I couldn't go home. I knew I'd done something wrong – I felt guilty and scared. I stroked the grey grass, pulled out a strand and ran the seed head between my finger and thumbs. The shower of seeds billowed out then blew back onto my navy coat. I left the path and wandered over the marshy area behind the hill where the marigolds grew. The dark grey of the horizon was spreading overhead. The heels of my shoes lodged in the squelchy ground then flipped back onto my feet. On a raised area of dry ground between the tussocks of bog grass I could see a small clearing. There was a rough nest made of spiky grass. In it lay four olive green eggs with charcoal freckles. I was dazzled. I could hear the triple scream of a curlew overhead. She circled until I walked back to the path.

Feeling dabs of rain on the back of my neck I pulled up my collar. I climbed down the ladder of stone steps and back onto the road. The road was clear so I ran across to my house and round to the back. Mum saw me though the window and opened the door.

"Where've you been?" she asked.

"Over the fields."

A man was standing in front of the blue kitchenette. I didn't know who he was. There was an uncomfortable silence. Then I recognized him – his round spectacles, his high forehead.

"I'll go now," he said. "I just wanted to let you know." Mum ushered him out of the door. When she turned to me I could see her face was pale with worry.

"I didn't know what had happened to you!" she said.

"How did he know where I lived?"

"He lives down Sussex Avenue. He's seen you playing in the garden."

"I didn't know what to do," I said.

Mum put her arms around me. I sobbed into her elbow.

"It's all right, love. It was an accident. As long as you're alright."

My brother, Warren, opened the back door. His knees were scabbed where he'd fallen off his bike.

"What's wrong?" he asked.

"Nothing," said Mum.

Mum had a black notebook which she wrote in if we'd been naughty. She showed it to Dad when he got home from work. If he thought Warren needed to be punished he would take him upstairs and hit him with the strap. I was never hit. When I heard Warren's cries I curled up on the floor of the living room and clenched all my muscles.

I told Dad about finding the curlew's eggs. He said that if a nest was disturbed too much then the mother wouldn't return. I went back to the fields a few times and searched through the bog grass. I couldn't be sure I ever found the spot where I'd seen the nest, but I never saw the eggs again.

Crab Apples 2

The crab apple tree in the garden stood next to a Siberian crab apple tree. Each year they both bore a faithful crop of fruit – one green, the other glossy crimson. Mum struggled with the tiny green apples to make jars of amber jelly.

I lay sunbathing in the lower part of the garden next to where we parked our touring caravan. I was building up a base tan for our holiday in France. Bees were making the most of the roses, and a gang of sparrows splashed in the pond. I heard the side gate click open and closed. My brother walked down the path and picked a couple of the green crab apples; the green ones were slightly bigger than the Siberian so had more weight. His aim was good. The apples stung my oiled arm and thigh. I chased him up the stone steps and into the house.

Warren was quicker than me and took the stairs three at a time. I saw him running from my bedroom to his. He slammed his door shut.

I scanned my room. I knew he'd taken something. Everything was in place on my bookcase. I kept my foreign doll collection on my chest of drawers. The Chinese girl was there in her red kimono, the Spanish couple flinging their arms in flamenco, the Welsh woman with her check shawl – the Russians, the Swedes, the Italians… But where was my Mexican in his sombrero?

I banged on Warren's door and pushed hard. He put his shoulder against the other side of the door and pushed harder.

"Give it back!" I shouted.

"What?"

"You know what."

"It's an 'it' now is it, not a 'he'?"

"You're not having your Beezer and Topper back now," I said.

"You've paid me to read them. You can keep them."

I banged and pushed some more then gave up.

"When Mum tucks me in at night I ask her who she loves best – you or me. She always says me," I said through the door.

"I ask her the same question. She always says me."

I stomped back to my room. The sun had gone in. I could see my striped beach towel on the grass from my window and the book I'd been reading lying open beside it. The breeze fanned its pages. I threw myself on my bed and stared at the ceiling. My bed was new. Warren and I had taken it in turns to stand on the end of my old bed and practice diving. One of the legs had split.

Downstairs Mum was in the kitchen making fly pie. I watched her while she piled the currants onto the round of pastry and poured over a layer of sugar. She gathered the edges of the pastry and stretched them over the currants, then welded them together and turned the whole thing upside down. She pressed the round down with her rolling pin to flatten it. The dark currants were just visible beneath the surface of the pastry, like tadpoles in a pool. As she painted the surface with egg wash I told Mum what Warren had done.

"He won't always be like this," she said.

"When will he stop?"

"When he's about fourteen," she said. "He'll be nicer then."

I didn't know whether to believe her, but she had an older brother so maybe she knew.

Stockings were never long enough. I had the longest legs in my year. I knew because we measured them in gym. We'd huddle in the cloakroom before going next door to the window bars, ropes and vaults. We stood side by side, lifting our games skirts and aligning our thighs. But where did legs begin?

The gap between stocking top and roll-on put more strain on the suspenders than they could take. Strands of vermicelli elastic would escape from the silky band at the top of the suspender. They'd fray and come astray. I hated sewing and mending, so I'd go to school with one or two suspenders missing. If the remaining suspenders were at the front, the stocking would gape down the back of my leg. I'd stand in the dinner queue and yank the stockings up, pulling great holes as my hands ripped through the flesh coloured nylon – American Tan, thirty denier.

One Tuesday I sighed at having ruined yet another pair of stockings as I stood in line for my portion of pink sponge with pink icing and pink custard. A turmoil of girls in varying lengths of navy pleats clattered plates, flicked food and slopped drinking water.

Tuesdays started off well – Bunty arrived in the morning. I relished the stories and the illustrations. Silvia was a window-dresser; Greta was a goalkeeper. Greta always saved the day for her hockey team at the last possible moment. I wanted to be a window dresser and a goalkeeper. There were abrupt headings at the top of each grid of pictures – 'Have you had your bicycle brakes tested recently?' 'Remember girls, never accept lifts from strangers in cars.' But I never got as far as cutting out Bunty's clothes on the back cover. The clothes were meant to be attached to Bunty's cut-out figure with fold-over tabs.

It seemed a precarious paper-thin way to dress her. And I could never figure out why the Four Marys were always in the third form at St. Elmo's. I meant to write in to ask but never did.

But Tuesday was also the day of my piano lesson. The thought made my stomach lurch. I enjoyed the theory. I liked to match the lines of words with the rhythm of notes. I remembered the Italian instructions – moderato, andante, allegretto. But I hated to play in front of my teacher. And more than that, I hated to play in front of a stranger for exams. I'd sit quaking in the cloakroom at the technical college feeling sicker and sicker. I'd be called to sit at a grand piano in a vast hall while the examiner lowered his bifocals and ordered scales and arpeggios.

I continued taking lessons, taking exams, sitting in Mr. Hamer's back room with its vase of dusty discoloured plastic flowers on the windowsill, its bust of Beethoven and the polished wooden metronome sitting on top of his upright. Mr Hamer (L.R.C.M., F.R.C.M.) was very conscientious. Even in a power cut we continued with a candle lighting the keys. But he loved tennis, and when Wimbledon was on he would slip next door to check on progress and scores while I prepared a piece to sight-read.

I sat on the top deck of the bus. It took me past my stop for home. It was two extra stops to Mr Hamer's. I sat in my blue uniform with grey felt hat. The grey hat which at first I'd been so keen to wear. Some girls from the convent sat behind me giggling. Brown uniforms and berets. They placed some lettuce leaves in the rim of my hat.

The bus pulled up at the stop I needed. As I stood up to go down the stairs I could feel both my remaining suspenders disengage. I stepped off the bus onto the pavement. Both stockings drifted down to my ankles. I wanted to slide down a grid. I hurried across the road to a doorway and pulled off my shoes and stuffed the stockings into my pocket.

I arrived at Mr Hamer's with bare legs and the lettuce still in my hat. We played Scarlatti.

Ruby and Maroon 4

I woke to rain thrashing against my window. Through the gap in my curtains I could see the low granite sky. I turned over and closed my eyes for a few moments. It was Saturday. Dad was downstairs, scraping a poker across the ashes in the grate.

I liked to touch the dimples and pimples on my wallpaper – to run my fingers over the blue daisy petals and the regular pattern of leaves. It was then I saw that the back of my hand was covered in blood. I sat bolt upright and pushed back the bedclothes. The sheets were stained with gashes of ruby and streaks of maroon. I ran into my parents' bedroom. Mum was sitting in bed, sipping tea; wisps of hair had strayed from her French pleat.

"My bed is full of blood!"

Mum's eyes searched mine. "We've been expecting this for a while."

Expecting this? How could they have been expecting a bed full of blood?

Mum opened the door of the white melamine wardrobe and delved into a huge Boots carrier bag. She gave me a packet of Dr White's sanitary towels and cardboard box.

"What are Dr White's?" I asked. "Is it a bra?"

"No it's not. Open the box."

Inside was a thin white circular band with two plastic hooks attached. Mum ripped a hole in the bag of sanitary towels and pulled one out.

"See, this goes round your waist. Then you fasten these loops onto the hooks like this." It looked very unlikely. "Why don't you have a bath and see what you can do?"

"Inside my knickers?" I asked.

"That's right. This will happen every month from now on."

I stared at her.

"What will?"

"A show of blood."

On Monday I took the bus to school. Before the conductor put the change in my waiting hand he ran his finger in four concentric circles on my palm then jabbed at the centre of the circle. I met his eyes then looked away.

The rain was back. At break time I walked into my classroom. Grace and Hilary were practising hurling insults at each other.

"You dirty cow," said Grace.

"You bloody bitch," said Hilary.

"You're a smelly spaz," hissed Grace.

"You're a stinking whore," snarled Hilary.

Their aggression alarmed me. I went to sit with Maureen's group in the other corner.

"It's alright, they're just practising," said Carol. "They don't mean it."

"It's a game," said Maureen. "They've been at it for ten minutes now."

"Are you OK?" asked Carol. "You look a bit pale."

"I've come on," I whispered.

"First time?" asked Carol. I nodded.

"You can get pregnant now," said Maureen.

"Can I?"

"Course you can. Didn't you know?"

I looked blank.

"Nobody's told her," said Carol.

She went to the satchel cupboard – a tall wooden cupboard by the door. The cupboard where last week we'd hidden Mavis just before our French teacher came in. She stayed there for the whole lesson, undetected. We were a pressure cooker of giggles. Carol rooted through her satchel and came back with a large science book.

"You'd better read Chapter 10," she said. "Take it home tonight. I don't need it again till tomorrow."

I opened the back door and stepped over the sheets of newspaper Mum had laid over her newly squeegied lino. She poured the dirty water down the sink.

"What are we having?" I asked Mum.

"Russian fish pie."

I was never quite sure what made it Russian.

"You left your sanitary belt and towels in the toilet this morning," she said.

"Did I?"

"Warren went in there and saw everything. I don't know what he made of it."

I took my shoes off and put them on the mat behind the back door.

"I'll go and do my homework."

Mum had cleaned and tidied my room, which I hated. I liked everything to be where I'd put it. I slid the science book out of my satchel and sat on my bed. *Chapter 10. Human Reproduction.* There were diagrams of a man's and a woman's reproductive systems sliced in half. *Oviducts, ovary, uterus. Sperm ducts, glands, testes (pronounced 'test-eez'). Sperm cells travel in semen from the penis and into the top of the vagina. The fertilized egg begins to develop into a foetus (pronounced 'fee-tuss').* This I could understand, but what I read next I couldn't believe. *Humans, pigs and dolphins are the only species who have sex for pleasure as well as for the purposes of reproduction.* So people went through this rigmarole even when they didn't want to have a baby? I was revolted.

"It's ready," called Mum from downstairs.

She sliced the envelope of puff pastry and spooned the creamy white sauce onto our plates. Gary Puckett and the Union Gap were singing *Young Girl* on the transistor radio. Something about being a baby underneath your make-up and perfume.

Mum looked at me from across the table.

"Every time I hear this song I think I should tell you the facts of life."

Mum made some of my clothes. I wasn't always grateful for this. I would stand at the edge of the dance floor at the Bury Social Club disco on a Friday night wearing a hot woollen fawn culotte suit, wishing I was wearing shop bought clothes. Dad would shoot me disapproving looks as Mum poured over the sewing machine and I expressed indifference to yet another outfit.

But there was one skirt she made which I really liked. It was a butter yellow and white above-the-knee gingham skirt cut on the cross. I took this skirt with me on our school trip to Stratford.

There were three of us sharing a room at the bed and breakfast. At the end of a day when we'd seen a production of 'Twelfth Night' and visited Anne Hathaway's Cottage we got ready for bed. I wound my hair around blue sponge rollers in anticipation of the following day.

A couple of hours after we'd switched the lights out the bedroom door opened and the light was switched on. Mrs Marshall, our English teacher, was standing at the door.

"There's three in here," she said to a woman standing behind her who I couldn't make out. She switched the light off and closed the door. I was mortified that Mrs Marshall had seen me in my rollers.

Samantha Entwistle had gone missing. There was a fairground in town. She'd been seen talking to the lad who swung the dodgems and she'd gone to meet him after dark. The next day, while the rest of us watched Hamlet, Samantha was sent home.

We thronged in the foyer at the interval. I was wearing my yellow gingham skirt. Carol came up behind me.

"You've started," she whispered to me.

"What?" I asked.

"You'd better go to the ladies. You can see it on the back of your skirt."

A patch of blood had spread across the yellow and

white squares. I didn't go back into the auditorium after the interval. I stood on the balcony and watched the tourists rowing along the River Avon.

That summer we took the caravan to Windermere. I knew my period would be due while we were away. I'm not using those sanitary towels any more, I thought. It's like having a hammock hanging between your legs. I packed a box of tampons, thinking if I only had tampons I'd have to learn how to use them.

A curtain divided the interior of the caravan into two rooms. The clouds hanging over the mountains hinted at their obscured contours. I tried to insert the tampon. It hurt like hell. Mum was waiting on the other side of the curtain.

"Mum, it won't go in. Will you do it for me?"

"I can't do that," she said.

5 Lady Macbeth

I loved Mrs Marshall. We all did. We wanted to be her. We wanted to be married to her husband and donate our trousseaus to the school play. We wanted a weekend cottage in Troutbeck, and to start our teaching careers in Wales. She wrote notes to herself on the back of her hand. When a member of staff came into the room we were quiet without being told. I never heard her raise her voice. We wrote poems together, we read Roman myths, we were the last year in our school to parse a sentence.

Each year we dismembered a Shakespeare play. In the first year we read *A Midsummer Night's Dream;* by the second year we were considered ready for tragedy. Books for the year were given out in the first English lesson of the term. Mrs Marshall placed my copy of *Macbeth* face down on my desk. I turned it over and filled in my name and form on the sticker on the inside cover. Above my name was *Sheila Standring LIVM 1963, June Heap LIVW 1964.* Underneath these names *Man from U.N.C.L.E.* had been written in pencil and then rubbed out. The words were lodged in the paper like letters drawn in wet sand. I'd carved *Illya Kuryakin* on my desk the week before and was given an hour's detention. The Deputy Head told me to sand down the desk lid and re-varnish it.

We were allowed to take our books home to back with brown paper. We didn't have brown paper at home so Mum helped me cut up remnants of anaglypta and bathroom washable. *A Tale of Two Cities* was covered with scenes from inland China. *From Flints to Printing* was clad in terracotta brick effect. I took the books back to school in my satchel to stack neatly along the bottom of my desk.

The hall was booked for our weekly Shakespeare lesson.

We congregated after the bell and waited for Mrs Marshall. Below the high ceilings of the hall were wooden panels and plaques listing in gold the names of old girls and their degree successes. A baby grand piano stood next to the stage. Our music teacher played Chopin, Debussy and Clementi as we filed into assembly. After hymns and prayers we listened to a sixth former give a reading from the bible. Then notices about sports results and societies followed. Once we were warned about putting sanitary towels down the toilet. I sat in horror. How could our Headmistress say those words in public? Our white-haired Headmistress who had never married because her fiancé was killed in the war.

Mrs. Marshall began to organize us in the hall.

"Get the benches out please, girls. Three in a triangle."

We dragged out benches from piles stacked at the sides of the hall and arranged them on a parquet floor. The parquet floor where we knelt at the beginning of each term to have the length of our pleated skirts checked. The floor where we stood waiting for assembly to start and whispered the latest gossip.

"Have you heard about Rosemary Smith? She's got to leave."

I didn't believe it. She was a prefect!

We sat silently on our benches. At break time I had sat silently with Carol and Maureen in a snigger over the desks in our form room. Maureen pointed to a worn page of the play.

"Have you seen what she says?"

"Who?" I asked.

"Lady Macbeth."

"Where?" said Carol.

"Page 66. And Page 71, that's even worse."

We read it over Maureen's shoulder and winced.

"I'm not reading that," announced Carol.

"Neither am I. No chance," said Maureen.

As we sat attentively Mrs Marshall asked who'd like to read parts. She cast the parts as we read scene by scene. First the witches, then the men with names like Scottish biscuit manufacturers – Duncan, Lennox, Donalbain. All hands shot up to read the King and Banquo. At the end of Act One, Scene Four there were five minutes of the lesson left.

"We won't start another scene just now," said Mrs Marshall. "But who would like to read Lady Macbeth next lesson?" A long thin silence zipped along the benches. Eyes dropped, legs crossed and uncrossed. The fingers on the clock ticked past the Roman numerals. Mrs Marshall looked around. Mrs Marshall who smiled and said hello to everyone, even off school premises. Mrs Marshall who was patient with late homework and ran the Busy Bee club for sick animals in her lunchtime. She must realize what she was asking someone to do? The silence grazed a little further. I couldn't stand it. I put up my hand.

At lunchtime, I stood with Carol and Maureen in the corridor. Our form teacher, Miss Bickerstaff, walked down the staffroom stairs. She had natural white-blonde hair and wore neat skirts. Her subject was Latin.

"I'm going to ask her," said Carol.

"Ask her what?" I said."

Miss Bickerstaff smiled at us as she walked by.

"Miss…?" said Carol.

"Yes…?"

"Can you tell us what a Latin word means?"

"What is it?"

"Coitus interruptus."

Miss Bickerstaff paused and scrutinized our facial expressions.

"If you promise to take it seriously."

"We will, Miss."

We followed her into our form room and closed the door. We left the room ten minutes later. I felt sick.

When school finished that afternoon I tucked my copy of tragedy into my satchel. I wasn't sure if my best friend was still my best friend so I didn't wait for her and walked to the bus stop alone. Valerie and I had started to be friends in the first year. One break time over the book cupboard she said, "I like you. Do you want to play jacks?" We played jacks endlessly – throwing the ball, snatching the metal stars with the same hand, then catching the ball on the drop from its bounce. I stuffed them back into my hand-made drawstring bag when break was over. Valerie came to my house, I went to hers. But then Jane came along and that changed things. Jane joined the class in the middle of the year. Valerie started to spend more time with her than me, and I pretended not to care.

At home I had tea with Mum and after written homework took the key to the caravan and went down to the garden. I hated caravanning. It felt like living in a vacuum flask. We would sit around the drop-leaf table listening to the rain pelting against the roof while the smell of the chemical toilet seeped from behind its door.

One winter's night the caravan was broken into while it stood at the top end of the garden on its concrete base. The next morning we found a sleeping bag from one of the cupboards curled up on the narrow bed. I was glad someone had stolen a good night's sleep.

Sitting at the table I looked at Lady Macbeth's speeches. I ran my finger along each line and read out loud until my intonation made sense of the words. I read slowly and deliberately. When I felt at ease with the words I closed the book, locked the caravan and went back inside the house.

"What have you been doing?" asked Mum.

"Nothing."

It was double English the next morning. When the bell sounded for the end of break my class ran along the corridors to the hall. We were told to "Walk, girls. Keep to the left." We dragged out the benches and were sitting squealing and shouting when Mrs Marshall appeared at the double doors.

"Girls, girls! The bell's gone. Other classes are trying to work." She paused. "Thank-you for getting out the benches. Let me see everyone sitting quietly." She paused again. "Good.

I haven't any home-work to return to you to-day so, Amy, tell us what's happened so far in the play."

Amy was quick with her answer.

"There's a battle, Miss, and Macbeth and Banquo come across three witches on a heath. They say that Macbeth will be king."

"Yes. Thank you Amy. Are we ready? Act One Scene Five." Mrs Marshall nodded towards me.

I read Macbeth's letter to Lady Macbeth and raised my voice slightly. At the end of the page everyone turned together. Even Mandy Bennett was on cue. She usually stared out of the window while we were reading. When the messenger arrived there were one or two shuffles as everyone sat up or leaned forward a little. Then the messenger left. I took a deep breath.

" 'Come you spirits
That tend on mortal thoughts, unsex me here
And fill me from crown to the toe top-full
Of direst cruelty. Make thick my blood;
Stop up the access and passage to remorse,
That no compunctious visitings of nature
Shake my fell purpose, nor keep peace between
The effect and it. Come to my woman's breasts
And take my milk for gall, you murdering ministers,
Wherever, in your sightless substances,
You wait on nature's mischief.' "

I could feel my neck redden. But my voice did not falter. We continued without discussion. At the end of Act One Mrs Marshall looked at me and said very quietly, "Good." She never gave easy praise. The class sat very still, and stared.

Paper

The secondary modern was further down the road from my school. Our sunken playground was below the level of the road. Passers-by peered through the black railings while we played tennis, pitched netballs, hung around at break time.

The Army Cadet Force from the equivalent boys' school opposite marched up and down the road weekly in their baggy khaki trousers and clacking boots. Boys from the secondary modern would stop and chat to girls through the railings.

I was leaning with one leg bent and my foot flat against the black stone wall.

"What's your name?" asked a boy with thick chestnut hair and olive skin.

"Chris."

"Aren't you going to ask me what mine is?"

"I suppose."

"Paul."

"Oh."

"Wanna go out?"

"Alright."

"Don't sound so enthusiastic."

"Well I don't know you."

"You soon will. Meet me at the youth club at 7.30 tomorrow night."

"OK."

"You'd better turn up."

The bell rang for lessons to start again.

The youth club was dark and dingy; the walls and ceiling were painted in rust-coloured gloss paint. There was a coffee bar, table tennis, pool, strip lights and low ceilings. Uncomfortable wooden seats like church pews lined the walls.

Paul nodded to me when he saw me. I walked over and stood by him, not knowing what to say.

"What's that?" I asked, pointing at a walking stick he was holding.

"You'll see. Want a coffee?"

He told me he was a catholic and he wanted to be a butcher.

"That way there'll always be meat to eat."

He showed me how to twist a sweet wrapper into a cup shape, spit in the base, and throw it up to the ceiling. The ceiling was covered with dozens of sweet-wrapper cups suspended on spittle.

"Where do you live?" I asked.

"On the council estate by the canal."

"I've been there on my bike."

He tore off a blank section of paper from one of the notices on the noticeboard and wrote down his address. I folded it carefully and put it in my jeans back pocket. Walking home he made sure he was on the outside of the pavement. His warm hand slid into mine.

Each time we passed a bus stop he lifted his walking stick and thwacked the bus stop sign. Each time we passed a row of railings he swapped sides and rattled his stick along their length.

It was almost dark as we rounded the corner to my avenue. A vast peach moon slipped in and out of the clouds. We stopped opposite at the end of my row of houses. Paul enveloped me and pressed his cushion lips against mine. He tasted good. We explored each other's cheekbones with our lips, the corners of our mouths, the silk of our eyelids. I heard footsteps marching along the opposite pavement. It was my father.

"Christine! Get in! Now!" he shouted. We sprang apart. My father crossed the road.

"I'll see you tomorrow," Paul said. "At school."

"The hell you will!" my father said.

As I walked to our house beside my father I looked three times over my shoulder at Paul. He waved. I didn't dare.

"Who's he?" said Dad as we stood in the morning room.

"He goes to the school near me."

"The grammar school?"

"No."

"The secondary modern?" he asked.

"Yes."

My mother stood silently by.

"Does he have any brothers and sisters?"

"Four brothers and three sisters."

"So he's catholic?"

"Yes."

"A left footer. I might have known."

"If you get pregnant," said my mother, "you can tell your headmistress." This was the nearest we ever got to a conversation about birth control.

"Don't worry, she'll not be seeing him again," said Dad. They went upstairs.

I took the piece of paper with Paul's address from my pocket and unfolded it. His handwriting sloped forward in faint pencil loops. What if my father found the paper and went round to his house? I opened the door of the central heating boiler. The burning coal smelled dry and acrid. I thought that if I threw the paper in the low flames Dad could still get the ashes out and identify Paul's address.

I went upstairs, tore the paper into twelve small pieces and lined them up on my bookshelf. One by one over the next few hours I put them in my mouth. I chewed and chewed then swallowed hard. I never saw Paul again.

7 Stepping in the Dark

At thirteen I wanted my mother to die. I woke up in a friend's dawn bed. The pain of the guilt cracked into tears. My friend woke up.

"What's the matter?" asked Janice. Janice and I were holiday friends. Janice lived in Manchester. We visited each other at Christmas and Easter. In the summer our families camped and caravanned together in Anglesey and Pwllheli. In term time we wrote to each other on pastel-coloured notepaper. I was staying over at Janice's for her thirteenth birthday party.

"I wished my Mum was dead." I sobbed bitterly, but thought I did not deserve any solace this confession might bring.

"Shhhhhh," Janice soothed, finding my hand under the covers. "It's alright. You didn't mean it."

And I didn't. But I didn't know that then.

Two months earlier I had woken in my own bed in the middle of the night. I could hear shouting. I pulled back a corner of the curtains. The crab apple blossom hung below my window like halted snowflakes. When this tree was in flower Mum called it my bridal bouquet. I had no intention of getting married.

"I can't do it any more!"

It was my mother I could hear shouting downstairs.

"And why do we never see your brother from one year to the next?"

Her voice was strained and several tones lower than usual. She sounded like a different person. I had never heard her shout before. I sat up in bed and pulled the cord on my reading light. My twelve foreign dolls on the chest of drawers looked anxiously across at me. The Spanish dancer with his arms outstretched, ready to click his castanets, cocked his head to one side. The alarm surfacing inside me made me sob.

"Maybe if they hear me crying they'll stop," I thought. The shouting carried on.

"And why didn't we get a wedding invitation from him? It was your niece's wedding!"

The event was three years ago. I could hear Dad speaking in gentle tones but I couldn't make out what he was saying. "If they see that I'm upset they'll stop," I thought. I climbed out of bed and walked to the top of the stairs. The carpet chafed my bare feet. As I went down the stairs I ran my hand along the raised surface of the bamboo effect wallpaper. The bumps and ridges were familiar to my fingers. The sitting room door was open. Mum was sitting on the two-seater lilac settee, her face a screw of tension. Dad was standing in front of the television, his arms folded across his wide chest. He looked tired and bewildered. I sat on the settee and took my mother's hand in mine. It was cold and clammy. I looked into my Mum's eyes and saw fear and anguish.

"It's all right Mum," I said, "God loves us."

I'd given up religion the previous year but it was the only thing I could think of to say. When I remember this night I realize it was the culmination of a series of peculiar incidents. A blue metal vase encircled with two snarling dragons had disappeared from the mantelpiece in the sitting room. A set of six silver teaspoons hanging on a silver stand had gone missing from the morning room. Both these items had belonged to my grandmother – my father's mother.

"Where did this vase come from?" I asked Mum one squally day when it was too wet to wander outside.

"Dad sent it back from India when he was in the forces. It was one of a pair. The other one never arrived. Your grandma gave it to me a year after we were married. Dad posted a couple of carpets too. God knows where they got to. She gave me those teaspoons as well. They've got an 'S' engraved on each handle. Did you notice? "

"Yes," I said. "Why do they have an 'S'? Our surname begins

with 'G'!"

"She won them in a tombola. A very posh tombola she would have me know."

"Did you like grandma?" I asked.

"She didn't like me. I wasn't good enough for your father."

"Why not?"

"Being pregnant with Warren didn't help. Your father didn't tell them. They found out from someone else. They wouldn't come to the wedding. Warren was four weeks old before they saw him. And then they only came because he was very poorly. Projectile vomiting. I could put a bucket at the end of the arc and catch it."

I'd heard this story many times.

I found the vase and the spoons six weeks later. Mum had hidden them in the cupboard under the stairs when she couldn't bear to look at them any longer.

The night before the shouting night my mother had gone next door to see the neighbours. She didn't usually visit the neighbours. Mr and Mrs Stumblich were kind enough. They had a son who'd been hit in the eye with a stone as he walked home from school. His left eye was now a ball of unmoving unseeing glass. Mum would tell this story to visitors – but this was the only way the Stumbliches usually featured in our day-to-day lives.

The day after the shouting was the last Friday of my Easter holidays. Mum ran outside into the street in her apron shouting, "Leave me alone. Leave me alone!" She refused to come inside. Standing on the opposite pavement she held onto the iron railings which were rooted in a low stone wall.

Dad grasped my arm and said, "I want you to go to the surgery. Tell Dr Stuart what's happened." I wanted to help but I was terrified. How could I explain to anyone what was going on? I ran to the bus stop and hailed the orange double decker. It drove past the park and the youth club, past the parade of shops with The Friary chip shop, and past the chiropodist where

I'd had my verruca removed. I got off at the stop outside the surgery. The receptionist sat peering out above her spectacles.

"What can I do for you?" she asked.

"Can I see Dr Stuart? …Please."

"Are you registered with him?"

"Yes."

"Do you have an appointment?"

"No." I panicked and blurted, "It's an emergency."

"Name?"

She scrolled in her ledger.

"Take a seat. Surgery's almost finished but I'll see if he can see you." She smiled warmly at me.

The receptionist didn't seem to think it was strange that I was alone, or if she did, she wasn't showing it. I sat down on a grey plastic chair. I was shaking. What was I supposed to say to the doctor? How could I convey to him how upside down everything had become? Time had taken on a new meaning, or no meaning at all. Everything was happening slowly at my house. Dad tried to do the cooking, but he burnt the lamb chops. We didn't see anyone from morning to day's end. And nothing actually happened. The grass didn't get cut, the car was dirty, the washing wasn't hung out to dry. I tried to steady myself by reading the notices on the wall. Heart Disease. Ante Natal Classes. V.D. Clinic. Then Dr Stuart appeared.

"Christine?"

Dr Stuart arrived at the house twenty minutes after I got back home. I saw his blue Rover pull up from the front window. Mum had come back as far as the garden wall but refused to go any further. He put his hand on her shoulder.

"Mrs Gittins. Hello. How are you?"

"Hello, Dr Stuart," said my mother brightly. "I'm very well. How are you?" He smiled at her and went inside the house.

"She doesn't sleep," said Dad. "She talks non-stop. She's raking up things which happened years ago."

"How long has she been like this?"

"A week… ten days. She won't rest. I can't get anything done." His tone was exasperated. I was sitting on the bottom step of the stairs. The front door was wide open so I could still see my mother. I was hurt by my father's disloyalty. Why was he complaining to Dr Stuart?

"You should have contacted me earlier. Can I use your phone?" The doctor made a call to the psychiatric ward at the local hospital. It was the ward where my mother had worked before she was married. Ward 17. Dad used to phone my mother there to ask her out to dances.

"It's Dr Stuart, I'm with a Mrs Gittins. No previous admissions." He made a stab at a diagnosis. "Paranoid schizophrenia." When I heard these words they entered my body and ricocheted like a pinball flipping against the four walls of a glass case. He put the phone down.

"There's a bed waiting for her. You can take her or I can call an ambulance."

"Does she have to go? Can't we look after her here?" Dad asked.

"I'm sorry, Mr Gittins. It's gone too far."

"I'll take her," said Dad. I was relieved. I couldn't bear the thought of an ambulance coming up the road to take Mum away.

The three of us persuaded Mum to come inside. She took her place on the settee.

"You need looking after for a while, Mrs Gittins. It won't be for long."

I wanted to believe him.

"I want to hear, 'What a Wonderful World.' Satchmo. He's my favourite," said Mum.

"I'll leave you to it, Mr Gittins. The hospital will keep me informed."

I opened the front door for him. I wanted to stay as long as possible with this person who seemed to understand what was going on.

Dad slid the record down the rod in the middle of the

radiogram deck and lifted the arm across. The speakers clicked when the needle hit the vinyl. Louis Armstrong's smiling voice sang of green trees and red roses.

The three of us sat on the lilac three-piece suite. I darted looks at my Mum, then at my father. The words from the song reverberated around the room... rainbow colours... pretty sky.

Mum was staring out of the window at the crab apple tree. The blossom was damp and heavy with rain. A single gust of wind sent a shower of petals spinning past the window. The record came to an end and the player clicked off.

"I want to hear it again," said Mum.

"We've got to go, love," said Dad.

"I want to hear it again," said Mum. There was something in her tone – a determined insistence, which made my father replace the arm on the disk. We all sat and listened again. Mum stroked the backs of her hands – three times on the left and four times on the right. She joined in with the end of each line of the song. I was glad when it reached its final repeated refrain: Armstrong thinking to himself about the wonderful world.

The player clicked off again.

"One more time," said Mum.

"Mum, it's time to go," I pleaded.

"After this," she said. "I'll go after this time." I set the arm on the disk and stood next to the gram, ready to leave. There was a family photograph on the sideboard. We were picking blackberries in Redisher Woods. Mum was holding up her juice-stained hands to the camera. I was brandishing a walking stick. Blackberry picking was something we did every year, in anticipation of pies and jam. I could almost feel the grit of the seeds in my mouth. When the last note of the song finished I switched off the gram. Dad held out his hand to Mum.

The following Monday I arrived at school late and tearful. I'd missed assembly and was hoping to slip unseen into my classroom. The building smelled of sawdust and disinfectant. A girl from my class was making her way down the same staircase.

"Are you all right?" she asked. It was Elizabeth Fell. We weren't particular friends but I respected Elizabeth. She seemed mature and worldly to me. In fact it was Elizabeth that I voted for as head girl four years later.

"My Mum's mentally ill."

"What's wrong with her?"

"She's having a nervous breakdown."

"A nervous breakdown isn't a mental illness," said Elizabeth. "She'll be alright." Elizabeth seemed to know what she was talking about, and I felt comforted. We both went into the classroom just as our Latin teacher arrived.

On my way home I climbed the stone steps into the public library. I walked around the shelves looking at the classifications – Natural History, Cookery, Philosophy. I knew that I needed psychiatry, that psychology explained what was wrong and that psychiatry cured it. There on the top shelf under the high window was the word 'PSYCHIATRY' printed in black letters and laminated onto yellow card. I ran my fingers along the titles. 'Psychiatry and Anti-Psychiatry,' 'Six Lectures on Psychoanalytic Psychiatry,' 'The New Language of Psychiatry.' I took the last book down off the shelf and looked at the contents page. Did my Mum have a neurosis or a psychosis? I didn't know. The book was complicated and technical. I replaced it in the gap on the shelf. Maybe I should study these subjects at university instead of the English degree I had planned.

It was lonely when I came home from school. Mum had always been there to greet me. We would eat together, exchanging the odd word. Sometimes I would read at the table. I knew I shouldn't but my mother never asked me not to, and I was always keen to finish my book. Dad was often late home and he would eat alone, waited on by my mother. Now when Dad came home he was invariably in a sour mood.

"What is this doing here?" he snapped, picking up some object which wasn't in its usual place. I would be cut to the quick. There was so much to worry about – I couldn't understand why he got so angry about such small things.

One evening as we sat together in the sitting room he talked to me in a way he never had before. "I should never have married your mother," he said. "I had plenty of girlfriends. I should have married Olwyn. She was a farm girl. Rosy cheeks and always smiling." I squirmed. I didn't want to hear he could have been happier with someone else.

Most days Dad would visit the hospital. Usually Warren and I went with him. For the first few days my mother railed at him.

"Why did you put me here? I want to go home. I want to go home!"

I would stand behind Mum's chair with my hand on her shoulder. I couldn't sit between my parents and listen to Mum.

The room was thick with cigarette smoke. Some patients sat in chairs, staring; some went about their business; and some stood or hovered, uncertain, like models about to adopt a pose. I remembered that Mum had worked on this ward. In the school holidays while we ate our dinner Warren and I would say to Mum, "Tell us a story about when you were a nurse." She would pause, then begin.

"I wore a dress with stripes. With a white starched apron and a cap. The doors of the ward were always locked in those days. Each nurse had a key. The sick ward wasn't supposed to be left unattended. But one day it was very hot and the side door was open. I was alone doing the dressing trolley. A patient ran out into the garden wearing only an open back nightdress. I ran after her. She stopped and put her arms round a tree. What a sight, poor soul. I helped her back to the ward. Then I was pulled over the coals by Sister for leaving the ward."

As the days went on Mum seemed more settled. She got to know the other patients. She enjoyed more company on the ward than she did off it. "I know all their stories," she said. She was an exceptional listener.

After her ECT treatments she'd be ashen and withdrawn. One Saturday afternoon there was blood on her cardigan. Her ear was ripped. "They pulled my earring. Yanked it out," she said, angrily, putting her lobe between her finger and thumb. "See? They split my ear." I was horrified. On the way out we looked for a member of staff.

"She was trying to escape," the nurse said, as though it was perfectly normal. I had never known my mother behave badly. "It was the fifth time this morning. I went to grab her and my hand caught her earring." It sounded perfectly feasible, but I didn't know what to believe. What if there was no end to the brutality of the staff after the visitors had left?

Six weeks after she'd been admitted Mum was ready to come home. On our last visit she accompanied us down the stairs to the exit door. She looked at the flower beds which lined the path up to the entrance.

"The roses are out. Pink and red. All in a line. Can you see that room over there?" she pointed across the hallway. "That's where I was given a party when I got married. All the staff came from Ward 17. *And* matron. They bought me a bedding box. The Lloyd Loom one in the bathroom. I painted it yellow."

Dad, Warren and I cleaned the house from top to bottom, and shopped for everything we could think of – boiled ham, stuffed olives, milk loaf. I waited at home while Dad went to collect my Mum, pacing up and down in the front room trying not to look out of the window too often. To distract myself I picked out one of the thick heavy seventy-eight records which were stacked on their sides in the radiogram. I made myself read every word on the middle of the disk. 'Dvorak's Humoreske, Opus 101, Number 7. Liberal Jewish Synagogue Organ, St. John's Wood, London.' The heaving organ began but there was a bad scratch across the disk – I tried to ignore it. Half way through the piece Dad's car drew up outside.

"They're here!" I called to Warren and ran to the door.

I put my arms round Mum and realized how thin she'd become. The drugs and the ECT had wrung her out. She was quiet, and when she did speak her voice was flat and empty of its usual warmth; her face was still. Over the next few days she took her medication and slowly picked up her chores – wiping dust from the leaves of the castor oil plant, stirring her soup on the electric cooker, wiping down the formica surfaces in the kitchen.

When I'd packed my bag to go to Janice's I'd put a troll on top of my clothes. Janice had a troll too. We spent hours combing their hair – stroking it, backcombing, plaiting, and tying it up with ribbons. Our trolls stood together on Janice's dressing table while I was getting ready for her birthday party. I tried to block out any thoughts of home. It was a relief to be in a household where everyone behaved how you'd expect them to.

The birthday buffet spilled over the dining room table – cheese and pineapple on sticks, pink cocktail sausages, bridge rolls with four different fillings, fairy cakes in paper cases and a white-iced Victoria sponge with birthday wishes piped in pink.

When most of it was eaten everyone was asked to congregate in the front room for a game. Janice's parents had arranged a line of objects in the middle of the carpet – a silver candelabra, a tall cut glass vase, a transistor radio, a newspaper rack, a table lamp, a wastepaper bin and a pot of pink lilies. Janice's father explained the game.

"I'll take one of you at a time and the rest can wait in the dining room for their turn. You'll be blindfolded and then it's my job to guide you. You have to step over the objects without knocking them over or even touching them. If you touch them then you're out. Janice – it's your birthday, you go first. And if everyone else can wait in the dining room please."

I went next door to wait for my turn. Janice's mother was emptying the table into the kitchen. There were crumbs and cocktails sticks scattered across the carpet. After a while I heard a yelp from the front room and then prolonged whispering.

"Chris, it's your turn now," called Janice. I went through and turned around so that Janice could blindfold me. Janice's father took my hand.

"We'll go over here to the start of the line. That's right," he said. "Now step forward just a little bit more. Now, lift your leg. Bit higher, just a bit more… that's it. Put it down. Now bring the other leg up. Down you go. That's it. Splendid. Now it's the glass vase, so we don't want to knock that over do we? Higher, bit higher. That's it. Well done. The transistor now – so small step. Easy peasy." He went on like this till I got to the end of the line. "Now the lilies. Last thing. We don't want soil all over the carpet so try your hardest. Higher… high as you can… bit higher. That's it. Terrific. You've done it."

I pulled the scarf from my eyes and slid it over my chin. I turned round to check that all the objects were still standing. But there was nothing there. The carpet was empty. Even before I'd taken my first step the objects had been removed.

Bucket

It was October half term. There were still discs of gold and orange hanging from the trees, all the more intense for their scarcity. I went into the sitting room, sat in the corner at the telephone table and dialled the number.

"Fairfield Hospital," said a cheery voice.

"Can you put me through to Ward 17 please?"

"Who would you like to speak to?"

"Dr Grimshaw."

"I'll put you through to his secretary."

Dr Grimshaw was Mum's psychiatrist in the early years of her illness. In the two years since her last episode his name hadn't featured in our house. We'd gone on with our lives without daring to look back. Now his name resonated again. Mum had started talking nineteen to the dozen, she wasn't sleeping, and she was going over and over the past.

"You went out with Ted Butler and left me at home. Night after night." Ted was an old friend and colleague of Dad's.

"That was ten years ago, love," said Dad.

Ordinarily Mum didn't complain about anything. Her illness seemed to be a bucket for all her resentments and hurts. Within a couple of weeks she was admitted to hospital again.

"Good morning. Can I help you?"

"I want to see Dr Grimshaw."

"Who am I speaking to?"

I said my name.

"Are you a patient of Dr Grimshaw's?"

"No, my Mum is."

"I see."

"She's on the ward."

"I'll check his diary." There was a long pause. "Dr Grimshaw could see you on Tuesday at 2 o'clock."

"I'll be at school."

"How about 4.30? Can you come then?"

"Yes."

"You know where it is, do you?"

"I've been before."

"Come to reception. It's all signposted."

"Thank you."

The sun threw boxes of light across the walls and furniture; it lit up the pattern of swirls on the lilac sofa. I fingered the valleys of the design. Dad came into the sitting room.

"Who were you talking to on the phone?"

"Fairfield."

"Why?" he said, taken aback.

"I want to see Dr Grimshaw."

"Why would you want to do that?" Now his tone was angry.

"I want to know why Mum is like this."

He walked out of the room. I went into the kitchen and looked at the long line of shoes on the doormat. Whenever I felt guilty about anything I would clean shoes. I prized the flat tin open with its metal swivel wing and used the stained duster to smear polish onto the leather. I brushed the toecap fiercely till it shone like a fresh conker. When I was half way down the line of shoes Dad came in from the garden. His hands were caked in soil and he'd brushed himself a scar across his left cheek. His eyes were sad and tired. He looked at the half line of cleaned shoes.

"I'd better come with you," he said.

On Tuesday Dad dropped me near to school as he usually did on the way to his office in Manchester.

"What the bloody hell are you doing?" he shouted at a driver who was sitting on his tail while he was waiting to reverse into a parking space.

I opened the door.

"I'll pick you up outside the main gate at 4 o'clock," he said. "OK."

The morning went quickly enough; it was double Geography in the afternoon, which I enjoyed. I liked the black and white photographs of physical forms in the textbook – drumlins and eskers, U-shaped valleys and oxbow lakes. We had a new teacher for Geography – Mr Marsden. He was recently back from Africa and would be teaching us for one term only before he returned. His hair was white blond and his eyes were the colour of a clear winter sky.

He'd been teaching us about rice production in Yunnan Province. This lesson we would be drawing maps and diagrams. Grace and Hilary sat at the back. I knew they had brown paper bags of pudding rice stashed on their knees. Mr Marsden drew a rice plant on the board.

He turned to us and pointed to the cluster of flower heads. "This is the panicle," he said then turned back to the board. Grace and Hilary each grabbed a handful of rice and aimed it at the back of Mr Marsden's head. Most of it skittered onto the floor, but some of it hit the back of his neck and slipped behind his collar, or bounced off his dark grey suit.

"Who did that?" he said, not quite firmly enough.

The Deputy Head was called and Hilary and Grace were frogmarched out of the classroom. Mr Marsden picked up a grain of rice from the floor.

"It's not even long grain rice!" he said and flung it in the bin.

Dad was waiting, as he'd said, in his Austin 1100. He looked solemn. In later years when Mum was hospitalised, after I'd left home, he'd drive to his office at the weekend just to clean the windows. His job was to inspect smashed up cars for insurance companies. Now he drove with the utmost care through the town and up the incline of Rochdale Old Road towards the hospital.

"Some people make a living out of people's good fortune.

Some people make a living out of people's misfortunes. I make a living out of people's misfortunes," he said.

I pondered this for a while.

"What are you going to make a living out of?"

"I don't know."

"You could be a lawyer. Or a detective sergeant."

I didn't reply. These were the people my father looked up to; the people who stood alongside him in court when he had to give evidence about an accident; the people who commanded authority, who were articulate, who had had an education beyond the age of fourteen. What impressed Dad was people who could talk.

He indicated to turn right into the hospital grounds.

"My Grandad used to say, 'Money's made flat for piling.' My Grandma used to say, 'Money's made round for rolling.' As long as you have enough of the stuff you'll be all right."

We parked in the car park which sloped up to Ward 17 and walked the flagged path to the entrance. Dr Grimshaw saw us in his dimly lit room. He was sitting behind a huge desk. Wisps of white hair from either side of his bald head sat on his ears. His gold half glasses were half way down his nose.

"Take a seat," he said, briskly. There were two upright chairs with leather seats placed at a safe distance from his desk.

"What can I do for you?" he asked. There was a note of impatience in his voice.

"I'd like to know why my Mum is how she is."

"Well, that's a very complicated question. We're doing everything we can for her."

"But she was here two years ago and now she's here again."

"Some psychiatric illnesses can be cyclical." I must have looked blank.

"That's to say they recur at regular intervals."

"But why does she get like this?" I asked.

"There's rarely one particular reason. There can be many contributing factors."

"I think it's because of my parents' marriage. Because of

their relationship."

Dr Grimshaw shot a look at my father.

"I think you've been reading too many newspapers," said Dr Grimshaw, crossly.

Dad remained silent throughout.

"We're doing what we can for your mother. She's comfortable and well looked after. Now, if you don't mind I have patients to see."

"I want to go and see Gordon," I said to Dad the following weekend.

"Why?" asked Dad.

"Well Mum keeps mentioning him. Maybe he knows why she gets ill." I thought there must be an answer, an explanation, a solution; that if we knew why it happened we could stop it happening again.

Ordinarily we didn't see much of Gordon. Dad and his brother were very different. Dad was fair and round-faced like his mother, Gordon was dark-haired and swarthy like his father. Gordon left home at the first opportunity, taking a job selling brushes door to door. Dad stayed on in Greenmount, and looked out for his parents. Gordon became a Labour councillor and ran a home for Mencap in St Annes. Dad voted Tory, started out as a mechanic, then worked with his father who managed a garage before joining a firm of consulting engineers. Dad married and stayed married. Gordon divorced, married again, and had a mistress. He sailed his yacht with his headmistress mistress. He said the best thing about her was that she was silent when they were at sea.

When Gordon visited his parents with Mim, his new wife, his mother put out three soup bowls instead of four. She proceeded to serve the soup while Mim sat at the table without a bowl. She took Gordon's wife shopping to buy a birthday present for my mother but she never bought Mim any kind of present at all.

Grandma and Pop moved near to us from Fleetwood when

they got older. Grandma was the first to die. Dad and Gordon decided to share looking after Pop – six months each. We did the first six months. Pop slept in the front room. I had to do my piano practice in front of him. He drank a bottle of brandy at Christmas and threw up in the waste paper bin. Gordon had an annexe built specially for him. Pop died just before he was due to move into it. He left three fifths of his money to Dad. Dad didn't want this and arranged for Gordon to have half.

Mum was close to her brother and sister. They visited each other regularly, they spoke on the phone, they had parties together. She couldn't understand Dad's distance from his brother. It disturbed her. Mum told me about Dad visiting his granddad. Dad was sitting up properly at the table. His Granddad took a gun out of a tin box and pointed it at Dad's head. Dad was six years old.

It was early evening. Warren and I sat in the back of the car. The sun was setting as we reached Middleton where Gordon lived. We saw an orange sliver on the horizon before it disappeared. Their house was called Redesmere. The yacht was pulled up on a piece of raised ground in front of the house. Before we opened the car doors we could hear Gordon playing his electric organ inside.

Dad and Gordon greeted each other.

"Can I get you a drink?" asked Gordon.

"What are you having?" said Dad.

"Whisky on the rocks."

"That'll do me."

What can I get you two?" said Mim. "Orange squash, lemonade, dandelion and burdock?"

Their house was opulent compared to ours. It was detached and had a small lake in the grounds. There were thick velvet drapes with drawstrings and tassels. On the dining table was a silver candelabra and a tray of silver goblets.

"How's Mary?" asked Gordon.

"Not too good," said Dad. "She's in Fairfield."

"And how's business?" asked Gordon.

"Pretty good. People will always drive their cars like idiots." Gordon laughed.

Mum wasn't mentioned again. When the conversation petered out Gordon sat down at his electric organ.

"I play every night," he said. "Till two in the morning. It keeps me sane."

He went through some of his repertoire – TV theme tunes, jazz, musicals, blues.

"Don't be a stranger," Dad said to Gordon as we left.

We visited Mum the evening of Warren's birthday. The four of us sat on a circle of grey plastic chairs in the Day Room. Mum spoke more to the other patients than she did to us. Then she showed us a picture she'd drawn. On the left was a tower of short horizontal parallel lines.

"That's Dad's paperwork," she said. "This is Warren's car," she said looking at him and pointing to a crossed-out car.

"I can't draw cars."

"Why did you draw these?" asked Warren.

"They asked us to draw what worried us." Mum gazed out of the window.

"Betty came to visit me this morning. Tom drove her up but he wouldn't get out of the car." Betty was Mum's younger sister. Warren and I would sometimes go to her house after school for tea when Mum was on the ward.

"We had Vera Duckworth in here from Coronation Street yesterday. She has a little friend in here she likes to visit."

A nurse rattled past with a trolley of medication.

"We'll go now," said Dad.

"I'll go and lie down for five minutes," said Mum. She gave a quick wave and shuffled towards the dormitory.

We drove to a nearby restaurant to celebrate Warren's birthday. There were only two other people in the dining room. We selected from the menu and I inspected my cutlery.

"Put it down," said Dad.

"Why?" I asked. "I'm seeing if it's like ours."

"It's not like ours now put it down!" Dad and I had been arguing from the moment we left the hospital.

The steaming plates of food arrived. Warren and I had chosen steak au poivre. Whole peppercorns were dotted through the creamy brown sauce.

"That doesn't look well done," said Dad, looking at my plate.

"I asked for medium rare," I said.

"I thought you said well done."

"Don't you think I know how I ordered my steak?"

Warren put down his knife and fork and blurted, "Shut up! Shut up! Don't you know? This is why Mum is ill!"

He got up from his chair, left the dining room and walked back to the car.

By February the following year Mum was home and she'd reached a hard won calm. I stood with my form and my year in Monday morning assembly. We listened to a sixth former reading a passage from The Bible.

"Psalm 15. A Psalm of David. Lord, who shall sojourn in thy tabernacle? Who shall dwell in thy holy hill? He that walketh uprightly, and worketh righteousness, and speaketh truth to his heart."

I dreaded the time I'd reach sixth form and would be asked to take to the stage and read extracts every day for a week. We sang, 'He Who Would Valiant Be' and as the last notes of the last verse hung in the Roger Kay Hall our headmistress, Miss Lester, walked towards the lectern. After the usual notices about games won and dates to note she paused.

"I'm afraid I have some very sad news. Some of you will know Lydia Porter from the Lower Sixth. She was involved in a car crash on Friday evening and I'm very sorry to say she did not survive. Our thoughts and deepest sympathies are with her family. A representative from the school will be attending the funeral on Thursday." Miss Lester looked down for a few moments, then raised her head again. "Now if you would file out very quietly please, we will continue our day."

I tried to fix Lydia's face in my mind. I could see fair hair and a soft face – was that her? Or did she have a thick dark plait and an aquiline nose? I wasn't sure.

By the time I reached our classroom I was weeping. I wept through algebra, I wept through French and I wept onto my painting of insects climbing through tall grass in my Art lesson. I didn't know why I was weeping. And neither did anyone else.

Mum was hospitalised every two years over the next ten years.

9   Praeludium and Allegro

There was only one male teacher at my school. Mr Bignall. Science. Tall. Withered. Beard. He had his own toilet. He picked his nose and flicked the contents. We called him Mr Pick-a-Fling. He was the only male teacher, that is, until Mr Creen arrived. Music. Young. Blond.

If I saw Mr Creen walking down the stairs from the music room and coming towards me in the corridor, blood would rush to my cheeks. I'd search him out in assembly to be able to see his soft features, his grey-blue eyes.

He gave a recital in the hall. He was a music teacher who gave recitals. We sat in attentive rows. The piece was introduced by our usual music teacher Mrs Milner. Praeludium and Allegro by Fritz Kreisler. Mr Creen put the bow to his violin. The notes soared high then low like a fickle winter wind. Mrs Milner added sturdy chords from the grand piano. The melodies climbed higher and the cadences swelled. I could see the undulating moors, rough rippling grass; the wind stung my face, made my sinews taut. I was shown paths I'd never trodden before.

"Are you coming on Saturday?" asked Wendy afterwards. Wendy lived in a lone stone farmhouse on the side of a hill in Norden. Her mother was throwing a party. She threw the kind of parties my mother never would. She invited teachers from school.

"I'm coming," I said.

Dad dropped me off at eight. I'd curled my hair, painted my nails and chosen an ankle-length floral dress stitched with orange ric-rac tape round the scooped neckline. The hall was the height of the house. A centre staircase split into an upper gallery.

Mr Creen was sitting by the stairs. All evening, at any opportunity, I gazed at him. He rarely met my eyes. His wife sat next to him.

Towards the end of the evening he grabbed my arm and pulled me into the cloakroom, shutting the door with his foot. He looked into my eyes and pushed me gently against the rows of coats hung against the wall. I leaned back into leather and wool.

"Is this what you want?" he said, kissing me fiercely.

He stood back, glared at me, then left.

10   A Small Smudge of Blood

The first time I felt a penis in my mouth was in a field on a Friday night. It was June. Martin had grown bored with my inexperience. Was I supposed to swallow it? It tasted bitter, like a milk pudding gone sour. His friends along the field heard it first – the grass had rustled. We'd disturbed a bull. The barbed wire was low enough to climb, but not to jump.

A week later we sat on his parents' settee. It was brown and itchy with black twists of wool growing through the cushions.

"I've waited three months," he announced. Was that how it was? Was I supposed to be grateful that he'd waited? I didn't know the rules. I didn't know there weren't any rules. I wouldn't have minded but it was his friend I fancied – Simon Christmas. He had thick dark curling hair, like a bending athlete on the side of a Grecian urn. Martin got to me first at a party. He had a beard. He had a job. He earned money – as a systems analyst at the C.W.S. building in Manchester. He sat me on his knee, pleased with himself.

"I can go to ten parties and not find anyone I like." I hadn't yet got the habit of parties.

At school I liked Art lessons best. It was the only time we didn't have to sit in silence. In Art we could talk behind our wooden drawing boards. We'd be painting on the theme chalked on the black board – 'Autumn Leaves' or 'Cats on Dustbins.'

"Mandy has," said Julie.

"No!" I said, amazed.

"So has Elizabeth."

"Elizabeth?" I was shocked. Elizabeth was my first choice for head girl. I didn't know if I could still nominate her now.

"Her and Barry have been doing it for ages."

"Where?" I asked.

"They drive to Ashworth Valley and walk for a while with a travelling rug."

I wasn't quite sure how much to believe. But as we scraped the hog hair brushes across the round blocks of poster colour we took a weekly tally. If what they said was true then I was in the minority. I would sit on the bus going home trying to imagine how it would feel to be one of the majority. How would it change me?

Meanwhile Martin and I sat on his parents' settee. He guided my hand to the mound in his trousers and unfastened his zip. The carriage clock ticked away on the mantelpiece. His parents looked out blankly from a gilt frame. 'Wedding Day' was written in sweeping arabesques of white ink along the bottom of the photograph. His mother looked particularly puzzled in her white veil and fitted frock. Afterwards Martin just sat and smiled at me for a long time.

A week later, along the railings near my house Martin pressed up against me. It was a chilly September evening and we had walked back from a pub in town. The iron bars made ridges in my back. Martin sighed deeply and pulled away.

"Let's get married," he said.

I didn't say anything. I was about to go to university. I couldn't marry a boy from Bury who proposed to me up against the railings of the Lido.

Martin buttoned his corduroy jacket and walked me round the corner.

In October I arrived in Newcastle with my trunk. My digs were on a bleak council estate in Denton Burn. I was sharing a room with Annie from Worcester who was studying psychology. We would lie on our small parallel single beds reading 'The Eye and the Brain' and 'Tamburlaine.' Outside dogs barked endlessly.

Our landlady was Mrs Gallon. Her husband was away at sea and she talked us to death morning and night. She cooked breakfast every morning with black pudding and fried bread, and she made our tea – plate salad with balls of cold potato mashed with cheese. By the second week I had fleas from Lucy the cat. It wasn't quite how Annie and I had envisaged university life. We began to skip tea and eat at the university refectory.

I didn't hear from Martin. After two weeks I chanced the rain one evening and stood in the dark in the only phone box on the estate. The raindrops on the glass drizzled into each other and ran the length of the window. I dialled the number. Martin picked up the phone straight away.

"I'm really glad you phoned. I didn't know what to say."

Why didn't he know? Did I know any better? We talked for a while till the distance fell away.

"I'm coming home in two weeks. For a weekend." It didn't seem too long to have to wait. I wondered what it would be like to see him, to feel the toughness of his beard, to have him want me again.

The journey home dragged. I phoned Martin as soon as I'd taken my bag upstairs. We arranged to meet the next day, Sunday. Then I realized that if I invited him for dinner we would have more time together. I asked Mum. She was peeling and coring apples in the kitchen. She looked up and paused.

"Go and ask your father."

I walked down the stone steps, past the frayed stumps of rhubarb, the dripping fuchsia and the late bitten roses. Dad was repairing the fence.

"Can Martin come for dinner?"

"No." He didn't even stop hammering.

I walked back to the house. Mum was lining a dish with pastry. The lino on the floor was newly washed and stuck with sheets of newspaper.

"He said, 'No.'"

Mum went on shaving the pastry from around the top of the dish. I went upstairs to my room.

If Dad wouldn't have Martin in the house then I would go with him outside the house. I packed my case and called him. When I heard the moan of his Morris engine I ran downstairs.

I didn't say goodbye to Dad. Mum stood in the hall, the white banister stretching up behind her, wringing her floury hands.

"Just drive," I said to Martin. He headed for Manchester where I could get my train. Mum and Dad never said they didn't like Martin. The only thing Mum would say was that she thought it was rude to walk into a room and switch on the television without asking.

We sat in the station buffet. Every few minutes a head of steam lifted from the silver hot water urn at the counter. I sipped my hot chocolate and looked at Martin. I'd wanted to see how it felt with him – then I would know whether to carry on. That 'No' of Dad's had brought us closer. I would go on seeing Martin. I would go on having a boyfriend at home. We found the platform and I found a carriage. Martin waved, unsmiling, as the train drew away.

It stopped at Staylybridge, Mossley, Greenfield, Marsden, and every station between Huddersfield, Leeds and York. The carriage was musty. The paintwork was dark brown and the seats were scratchy. Above the seats the lights flickered three times then died. As the train rushed through the darkness and the scattered lights of kitchens and petrol stations I sat upright, expectant. Annie and I were planning on leaving Mrs Gallon's. We were going to get a flat-share. I would ask Martin to come and stay. It was time. I wanted to know.

Annie and I found a postcard on the Union building noticeboard – an upstairs flat in Heaton. It was on the top floor of a red brick terrace – dark and narrow with turquoise woodwork on the landing. There were three bedrooms – medium-sized, very small and even smaller. Dave and Anna, who had advertised for sharers – third year French – had the larger room. They pushed their single beds together and asked the landlord for a double. It never arrived.

Though strangers to each other we lived communally, taking turns to cook in the evenings. Anna grated carrots for râpée, Annie added double cream to macaroni cheese to make it 'de luxe,' I made chilli con carne with tins of baked beans.

My room was loaded like a furniture van. Piles of clothes marked out the purple carpet. I tidied up for Martin.

We met at the station and went across the road to Yates's Wine Lodge. The bar was loud and dense with smoke. Men who'd left their homeland and families to build roads and bridges were singing in Gaelic and reeling towards the bar. We drained our sweet syrupy wine and walked the shiny streets to the bus stop.

The flat was quiet. No one was back. We made tea in heavily patterned mugs and went to my room. Without speaking we undressed ourselves and lay down facing each other on my narrow bed. Too soon he came inside me. For a moment I felt filled up, complete, but none of the sensations I'd been expecting. He pulled away from me and slept. I lay awake, not understanding.

As we walked round W.H. Smith's in Eldon Square the next day I remembered the night before. There'd been a slight rip of pain, then a gash of disappointment. I needn't have waited. After Martin left I cut out a square of the bed sheet where there was a small smudge of blood. I kept it in a pale blue jeweller's box along with an old eye tooth and a locket I'd been given as a bridesmaid.

The Swiss cheese plant in the morning room was breaking loose. I'd persuaded Mum to buy it, along with a rubber plant for the front room. The rubber plant had reached the ceiling, and the Swiss cheese plant had colonised its corner, sending out aerial roots in all directions.

I sat at the blue formica table and fiddled with the metal hinge underneath which held up the drop-down leaf. It was early on the second Saturday of my first Christmas home from university.

Everything was the same – the view over the fence to the tennis club and the low-lying primary school, the pond in the garden surrounded by flag iris and Mum's plaster of Paris rabbits made from jelly moulds. The goldfish were suspended in a deep block of ice, destined to maintain their position until the temperature rose.

I'd signed up to deliver the Christmas post, along with many other students who were home for the holidays. The day before, my postbag had weighed heavy on my shoulder. I walked from the bus stop up to my round in Walmersley and Nangreaves. The bag-strap dug into my shoulder and the bulk of envelopes banged against my hip as I walked. I could carry it no longer. I let the bag slide off my shoulder, dropped it by a long wall which ran in front of a row of blackened stone cottages, and pulled out the envelopes for those doors.

When I'd finished the posting and walked back to the end of the wall the bag had gone. I stood for a moment, not knowing what to do. The door to the first cottage opened. A grey-haired lady came down her garden path towards me.

"Have you lost something?" she asked.

"A post bag," I said. "With post in it."

"You'd better come in." I followed her up the path.

The bag was sitting in her porch, underneath a shelf of geraniums.

"I got the shock of my life," she said. "I was on my way back from the shops. I had to come in and have a brandy. I phoned the post office. They asked me to look out for you." She did look pale.

"It's so heavy," I said.

"Well of course it is, it's got all our Christmas greetings in it!"

I took the bag and went on my way.

I slid my fingers across the leaves of the Swiss cheese plant. Mum oiled the leaves every few weeks. She was stacking oxtail and butterbeans in the pressure cooker in the kitchen. When she'd finished chopping onions and carrots she came and sat with me. I couldn't look at her. My insides were twisting with grief. I put my head in my hands and wept.

"What is it?" Mum asked, anxiously. I didn't answer. The tears kept coming. Mum put her hand on my knee.

Dad came in from the garden. I could feel him standing near me.

"What's to do?" he said. I didn't think I knew.

"You don't know what's been happening to me for the last three months," I said.

Their life in Lancashire had been going on in parallel to mine in Newcastle. Mum had been polishing the brasses and bottoming out her cupboards; Dad had been going to his office, visiting garages and coming home to cheese and onion pie and rice pudding with a skin on top. I'd found the far reaches of the university library, got to grips with Descartes and Chomsky, and seen a student with red hair set fire to himself on the Union steps in the name of the coup in Chile.

My weeping subsided.

"I'd better go," I said. "I'll be late for my round."

Mum looked bewildered. Dad helped me on with my coat.

"Wrap up warm," he said, 'it's started snowing."

I reached the beginning of my round on the council estate at Walmersley and the snow started blizzarding. At first I could see four houses in front of me, then two, then one. The wind cut into my cheeks and the snow rested on my gloves. I waited till I was under the canopy above each front door before I took the hand written envelopes out of my bag.

As I was rounding the corner to the stone cottages I could see a figure coming towards me through the swirling flakes. The grey mass solidified and I could see a man in a peaked cap. It was my father – his cheeks as ruddy as mine. He was smiling broadly.

"Give me some of those envelopes," he said. "We'll do it together."

We worked our way round the streets until the bag was empty.

Martin and I were due to see each other. There was an

afternoon when my parents were going to be out.

"You know why I'm coming round don't you?" Martin said. It felt like a threat. We lay on my childhood bed and he came in my hands.

"Sorry," he said, "I got too excited."

Downstairs we began to kiss again. Between the settee and the armchair, on the floor of the sitting room, I began to feel pleasure. He held me hard against him until my shudders subsided.

Seven days later my period was due. I sat around the house with a jab of anxiety in the pit of my stomach. Every half-hour I went to the toilet to check.

"What's the matter?" asked Mum.

"Nothing."

Martin seemed unconcerned. This had happened to him before and the girls were never pregnant. He was beginning to think he might be infertile. I think he wanted me to prove him wrong. I began to hate him.

After nine days I started to bleed. In the relief I told Mum what had happened.

"I know," she said. The same thing had happened to her, except that she *was* pregnant. She married under a girder of disapproval. She married in a powder blue barathea costume with a white satin hat and tan shoes. There was a spray of orchids in her lapel. They didn't tell the staff at the hotel in Morecambe that they were on honeymoon, but Mum said they knew, because at breakfast she had to ask Dad if he took sugar in his tea.

I never saw Martin again. That January he sent me a present for my birthday – the Penguin Book of English Romantic Verse. In it he wrote that I was full of romantic images, too full for him; he hoped I liked the book and that I hadn't got it already.

The day I got back to Newcastle for the spring term I made an appointment at the university clinic. I wanted family planning, without the family.

11   Red Leatherette

Gerry Musgrove was already in trouble with my father because he'd borrowed a sleeping bag when he fell out with his parents and had never given it back. He slept in his car for a week.

He was one of my brother's friends. And it wasn't as though I really liked him. But he dared me. We were sitting in the Odeon in Bury on a Saturday night. The Odeon where I'd worked as an usherette during my final school holiday; where the heating was turned up at the interval to encourage the sales of ice cream; where I'd learned that there were two prices for the ice creams – one for when the manager was around and one for when he wasn't. The permanent usherettes pocketed the difference. They'd pour the coins onto a table and slide the difference into their pockets. It was like the seaside slot machine where pennies drip from one rotating shelf to another and slip down a chute.

There was a gang of us in the cinema. Gerry was sitting next to me. He was broad shouldered and his skin was made paler by the blue-blackness of his thick hair. He started by putting his arm round my shoulder. With his other hand he took my hand and placed it on his thigh. He didn't turn his head, but looked resolutely at the screen where Paul Newman was swindling Robert Shaw in a double bluff poker game on a swaying train. He *did* look at me once, and smiled, when Newman and Redford wiped away their fake blood as they sat up on the floral carpet of a Chicago drugstore.

The credits began to climb the screen. Gerry leaned over and caught my mouth with his. The gentle pressing of his lips gradually increased in pressure. He pulled away.

"I dare you to come to Manchester with me. Stay overnight

in a posh hotel."

Mum was in hospital again. It was the middle of the university summer holidays. At home each room was spun thickly with webs of claustrophobia.

"I bet you're too chicken," said Gerry.

"I bet you I'm not. You're on."

Gerry picked me up the following Saturday. I'd packed my cream vanity case with what I thought I might need. Dad was cleaning the brasses in the breakfast room. The horse brasses, candlesticks, teapot and the miniature bedpan were lined up on the table waiting for their coating of Brasso.

"You look all dolled up. Where are you off to?"

"Manchester."

"Who with?"

"Gerry Musgrove." Dad raised his eyes to the ceiling. The week before Dad had set an alarm clock off outside the door of the front room when he thought Gerry had outstayed his welcome.

"Where in Manchester?"

"We're going for a meal."

"You can have a meal in Bury!"

"I know."

"Don't you think you should put some more clothes on?"

"No." I left the room.

"Don't be late," he called after me.

I slammed the back door.

Gerry's Datsun smelt of earth and peppermint.

"All right?" he asked as I moved a pillow from my feet onto the back seat.

"All right," I replied.

Gerry was partly responsible for embezzling the sports fund at Bury Technical College – money used for expenses when teams played away. He'd been found out and had paid back his share.

"I'll pay for everything," he said, with bravado.

"No you won't."

He drove at speed between one set of traffic lights and the next, along the road which leads from a small town to a large city – Prestwich, Heaton Park, Cheatham Hill, and finally Piccadilly Gardens. We parked up and Gerry held the door open for me.

"Madam!" he said, standing to attention like a chauffeur.

"I thank you, Sir."

He took my hand as we walked up the steps of The Quest Hotel. The reception desk was cushioned with a bolster of red leatherette. There were rows of lights hanging from the ceiling; the light bulbs were hidden amongst long strips of translucent dripping purple plastic.

"Do you have a booking at all, Sir?" asked the receptionist.

"Yes. In the name of Musgrove."

"Oh yes. You're in Room 37. If you could sign here, please Mr Musgrove." Gerry shot me a mischievous look before he signed.

"Would you like any help with your luggage?"

"No thanks," said Gerry, grabbing my vanity case.

"This is your key. If you could please leave it here at reception when you're not actually in the hotel."

We called the lift.

"Does he think I've not stayed in a hotel before?" said Gerry, indignantly.

"I haven't," I said.

Our room was three floors up. The window looked out onto a blank brick wall. I stroked the beige polyester curtains. Gerry sat on the edge of the bed then fell back and bounced.

"I think it's one of those orthopaedic mattresses," he said, as I inspected the bathroom.

"There's a nice shower cap in here for you."

"I don't bother with those."

"I didn't think you would."

In the bedroom I busied myself with the chest of drawers.

"Hair dryer. Gideon's Bible. Tissues."

"Come over here," said Gerry.

"I'm hungry. Let's go for something to eat."

He tried to grab my hand and pull me to him. I slipped his grip.

"OK. Have it your own way."

We found the hotel restaurant and slid into a green banquette.

"What do you fancy?" said Gerry, handing me the menu. "Apart from me, of course."

"Something meaty."

"That'll be me then!"

"Give over, Gerry."

"I'm having steak," he said.

"Me too."

"How do you like yours?"

"Medium rare."

"I'm a well done kind of guy."

"Funny, I can't see your sun tan."

"Yeah – funny," said Gerry with a sneer.

The waiter poured a little of our chosen wine into Gerry's glass. Mateus Rosé.

"Yes, that's fine," he said.

"Why didn't he pour some into my glass?" I asked, after the waiter had gone.

"Because I'm the expert."

"As if."

As I cut into my bloodied sirloin I could feel the weight of our room above, waiting for us to finish. Dread crept into me like a virus from a sneezing child. Our banter abated. We ate desert in silence.

"Shall we go up?" asked Gerry, unceremoniously. I nodded.

When I pulled the curtains together in our room they didn't quite close. The acid yellow of the street lights seeped around the edges.

We undressed and pulled back the bedclothes. Gerry touched me as though I were a car engine – checking in with the different components and rotating his attention until I was breathless. When my moans accelerated he came quickly. His body went limp on top of mine and he fell asleep. I rolled him onto his back and he sighed deeply. For a while I lay listening to the drone of traffic in the street, and the rain fingering the window.

When I woke Gerry was still snoring gently. I crept into the bathroom and got dressed, picked up my shoes from the stained carpet, and gathered my jewellery from the bedside table. The door clicked as I closed it.

Outside there was still a lick of rain on the pavement, but the air was clear and the sky had lifted to blue. I walked through the Sunday city – around the circularity of Manchester Central Library, and past the enticing clothes shops of King Street. At Victoria Railway Station I bought a one-way ticket to Bury.

Bowker Vale, Heaton Park, Bessies o'th' Barn. As the train stopped at familiar stations I remembered journeys home from Manchester on Saturday nights when I was still at school. After dancing for hours to Deep Purple and Marvin Gaye in murky nightclubs my friends and I would pile into the carriages of the last train home. Someone would smash the light bulbs, then all the boys changed seats so they were sat next to a girl – any girl. The point was to have someone to kiss for the length of the journey – it didn't matter if you'd never seen her before.

From Bury I took the bus to Walmersley and walked the length of Mosley Avenue. Our semi-detached house stood at the end. 'South' and 'View' were carved into the columns on either side of the front gate. Mum's carefully tended roses were blooming cerise and magenta in the four symmetrical beds by the side of the house. There was a row of upturned grapefruit skins waiting to catch slugs.

I opened the back door. Dad was standing by the window in the morning room with his arms folded. He looked angry and hurt. We didn't exchange a word. I went upstairs to my room.

In the recess by the stone fireplace Mum kept a framed photograph of herself. She was in her early twenties, sitting with her legs stretched out on a beach towel – lithe, tanned and relaxed. Behind her rise the dunes and marram grass of Formby. She is wearing her brown and turquoise harlequin shorts, which still lay folded in her ottoman, and a V-neck white sleeveless top slipped over her shoulders. Her brilliant smile is the smile of a young woman who has time to be warmed by the sun, to waggle her toes, and finger the leaf motif on her towel whilst her handsome young man focuses the camera.

"I look at that photograph sometimes while I'm sitting here," she said. For the first time I had the sense of her life being arrested whilst she took a backward glance; was it with regret, with yearning?

"I can't sit in the sun now. Because of the lithium." I didn't know what to say to this pleasure chipped away. She also couldn't take strong painkillers for her osteoarthritis for the same reason.

It was a cold damp September day.

"There's not much sun today," she said.

"The days are getting shorter," I said.

"I could do with a piece of elastic on each day. I'll pull some out of my knickers."

I got up to go to kitchen.

"I'll make some tea," I said.

"There's Eccles cakes in the tureen."

"The green Poole Pottery one with the mushrooms on the lid?"

"That's the one."

Through the kitchen window I could no longer see the thick

hedge of rhododendrons which had separated my parents' garden from the one beyond. The new neighbours had sheared down the bushes to claim back their boundary, without a word to my parents. They'd lived with those luxurious lavender blooms, and the promise of them, for over a decade. Now they were replaced by dull two-dimensional featherboard fencing. Mum's only comment had been an enthusiastic one:

"They've got a designer garden! You can see it through the trellis. Have a look!"

There were cordylines and cannas growing at intervals between gravel and paving.

I took the tea through. Mum was squirming in her chair.

"I've got thrush," she said..

"How are you treating it?"

"With calamine lotion. I'm wearing two pairs of knickers and a pantie girdle."

"Don't you need to let the air in?"

Mum didn't answer.

"Is your new television all right?" I asked.

"Yes, it is. We're very pleased with it. But I don't think that Kate Adie's ever coming back. She's always at some war or other."

"Have you been watching 'Portrait of a Marriage?'"

"Oooo yes!" said Mum.

"Janet McTeer is very tall isn't she?"

Mum nodded.

"It made me think I should have a pair of jodhpurs. So I went in that riding shop in Bridge Street."

I'd picked up my Eccles cake but I put it down again without taking a bite.

"You didn't! The one with the full-sized horse in the window?"

"They didn't have my size, so I bought a red waistcoat instead," she said, triumphantly.

"So now you've got a red waistcoat, red boots and a red hat!"

"And a red handbag."

Mum took a gulp of tea.

"I left Dad walking up and down Bridge Street. He was proper blazing when I came out."

"Oh dear. Were they nice in the shop?"

"She asked if I had a horse."

"What did you say?"

"I said I borrow one. Then she said was I interested in things equestrian?"

"What did you say?"

"I said I just cantered."

"Mum!"

I picked up my Eccles cake again.

"I can't believe you."

"It's true."

"I do like listening to the sound of your voice. Apart from what you tell me," I said.

"I was told once I had timbre in my voice."

Dad came to join us. As he fell back into the sofa his legs flew up in the air.

"Steady," said Mum.

"Is there a cup for me?" he asked.

"Here. There's your favourite, Dad – Eccles cakes," I said, handing him a cup and a plate.

"He struggles a bit now with his false teeth," said Mum.

"I had cheese and biscuits the other night," he said. "It was like eating a grand piano with the lid up."

They lived under permanent siege. The bungalow was in the corner of a cul-de-sac. Each time a car drove by they checked to see who it was. Each time the security light came on at the front of the bungalow they checked for prowlers. Each time there was a noise they didn't understand Dad would jump up to see if it was a cause for concern.

"Do you still go to your Masonic meetings, Dad?"

"No. I don't like to leave your Mum."

"You've been to one or two!" said Mum, indignantly.

"I remember going through the ottoman when I was little and coming across your Masonic apron in a leather case."

"Yes, and you didn't put it back properly," said Dad.

"You knew?"

"Of course I knew."

"The Masons!" said Mum. "I've had more support from my knitting group!"

"And I found some rubber tubing with a rubber balloon at the end," I said.

"That was for expressing milk," said Mum.

"Oh, is that what it was. I thought it was some early form of contraception!" Dad laughed.

"We've been married for 40 years now," said Mum, with pride and disbelief.

"I think we've learned compassion, and how to look after each other," said Dad.

"There's things I think we'd both have changed. Dad worked too hard, and I could have had a career."

"Did you feel as though you were pushed into having to look after children?" asked Dad.

"No. I enjoyed that. But after they left home…"

"Twenty years ago now," Dad said, wistfully.

"We talk more now."

"I can't imagine being with anyone but your Mum."

A gust of wind rasped through the beech and hawthorn trees in the garden.

Dad pulled himself up off the sofa. He collected the crockery onto the tray and ate a stray currant from the Eccles cakes.

"I'll do the washing up."

After he'd closed the door to the room Mum said conspiratorially, "I didn't tell you… he's getting very forgetful." She paused. "Anyway I never met anyone else. I've not even been away for a weekend on my own."

In the evening Mum would fall asleep first in her chair, followed by Dad. They'd wake and drop off, wake and drop off.

"Is it time for bed now, Mum?" I'd ask.

"Just a few more minutes. It's only nine o'clock. Have I missed Coronation Street?"

"I'll go and get ready," Dad said. "Are you coming?"

"In a minute," said Mum.

When she eventually got up from her 'ejector seat' her parting shot was, "Don't stay up all night watching films." I think she would've liked to stay up late watching films.

After I switched the T.V. off I sat for a few moments listening to the wood pigeons calling from the copse.

There was barely any light in the sky when Mum came into my room the next morning. It was the room which Mum and Dad had shared, until Dad began reliving World War II in his sleep. He would shout and wail, his arms would flail and he frequently threw himself on the floor. So Mum took cover in one of the two smaller bedrooms, and Dad slept in the other.

Mum was standing at the foot of my bed looking pale and tired.

"I've been up all night playing Russian roulette!"

I pulled myself up on my pillows.

"I went to bed and that light kept flashing." There was a second security light outside Mum's bedroom window. It could be activated by a passing cat or by the wind.

"It was like a disco in there. So I went into Dad. We changed beds. He couldn't sleep either. So he switched off the electricity! I get up to go to the toilet and make a cup of tea and there's no light. And the freezer's off, and the fridge. So I wakes him up again. 'What have you done?' He gets up and switches the electricity back on."

"Oh Mum." She came and put her arms round me.

"Do you wear a bra in bed?" she asked.

"No."

"I do. It keeps your bosoms right."

Later that morning Dad and I took to the hills. We drove up Rawson's Rake in low gear, parked by Emmanuel Church and walked along Moor Bottom – the path which skirts Holcombe Hill; it runs between stone cottages with mullioned windows before leaping out onto the moor. To the right the flank of the hill shimmered with grass tussocks tousled by the wind. To the left the valley swept down through emerald fields and up to the raw slopes of Ashworth Moor and Scout Moor. In the summer there were dashes of royal blue through the grass where patches of waving harebells grew. Now the winberry leaves were reddening and heather spread cushions of mauve across the hillside.

"Can you hear the skylark, Dad?"

"Yes. Can you see it?"

"Just about. It's over there above the tower."

"Too far away for me."

"Did you used to come scrambling here?"

"Yes. I'd go home covered in mud from top to toe."

We leaned over the drystone wall and looked at Manchester far off in the distance.

Just before I left to go back to London Mum gave me two covered coat hangers, two Crown Derby teacups with hairline cracks to put plants in, and a travel sewing case.

"That'll do for your transatlantic trips." There were tears in her eyes.

Dad drove me to Manchester Piccadilly. I played him my new Jessye Norman tape. As we traced the familiar route George Gershwin's lyrics slipped out of the windows onto the M66 motorway.

Dad sang along softly.

"Our love is here to stay."

He struggled to find fourth gear.

"This was our song in the blitz."

There was a break in the clouds; a spotlight of sunshine shot across the moors. In seconds the clouds closed together again.

We were in good time for the train so we sat a while in the car. Dad was quiet at first; he played like a child with the objects in the car – opening a tin of change and turning a screwdriver through his fingers.

"It's good to see you, Dad."

His eyes filled with tears.

"I get frightened," he said. "Of having a heart attack." He looked out at the cars arriving and departing then looked back into my eyes. "Just give me five more years."

I didn't know what to say.

"Would you like to borrow my Jessye Norman tape? A Norman for a Norman?"

"Yes please. Would you like to borrow 'Yes Minister'?"

"Yes please."

A week later, back home, I was running a temperature. I lay propped up on a pile of cushions on my blue water silk sofa. The phone rang. There'd been a few calls that week when no one had spoken. My answer machine was broken. Half asleep, I picked up the phone but didn't say anything in the hope of flushing out the mute caller. I listened a while and whoever was at the other end put down the phone. Straight away the phone rang again. I picked up but didn't speak. The silence was longer than before, then the phone was put down.

Twenty minutes later the phone rang again. This time the silence stretched into minutes and the deep breathing began. The phone went down. I called the operator to ask about having my calls screened then went back to sleep.

That evening Mum phoned.

"I tried calling you this afternoon. Three times."

"Why didn't you speak?" I asked.

"I was waiting for your answer machine."

"What've you been doing?" I asked.

"I went to bed today."

"Why?"

"Because I wanted a change."

"Oh."

"Are you all right?"

"Stop worrying. I'm alive aren't I?"

"Yes you are!"

"I'll probably think of something to say to you when I put the phone down."

I phoned Mum on her 67th birthday; it was a wet day in April. She'd opened her cards and presents at 2.30 that morning.

"I got your card and letter, thank you," she said. "It's like 'Forthcoming Attractions'!"

"Well Happy Birthday, Mum."

"When I was born I was born on a board," she said. "I was born on a board with a cobweb over my head. George Formby had a cobweb too."

"Did he now. What have you been doing?"

"I've been chasing a duck round the garden. And I've just had a bath. I look like a walrus."

"Is it dripping on the carpet?"

"It's only water," she said.

I'd been invited to the Troubadour Coffee House in West Kensington to read some poems.

"When I do my reading, Mum, I'm going to start with two poems inspired by you."

"What is it? A recipe?"

A month later she disappeared half way through breakfast. She did some shopping in Ramsbottom, bought a present for her grandson, and took a taxi to Ward 17 at Fairfield Hospital. Earlier in the year she'd been due to have a minor operation; in preparation she was taken off her lithium. She caught a chest infection and the operation was delayed. When she recovered from the operation lithium was not re-prescribed. By July she had been admitted to Ward 17 three times that year.

She called me from the ward one afternoon. Her voice was gentle and calm, her speech a little rushed.

"Did you know I was in here? I came in on Monday. It's very

hectic, very busy. Chiropody appointment, tummy, mouth, do I want a haircut… ? I want rubbing out and drawing again!"

There was a pause.

"Dad came to-day."

The night before Dad told me she had hit him when he visited. He said it didn't matter. She couldn't get the money in the slot. She went downstairs to get her purse. My phone rang again.

"Sorry, I'm a bit slow. It's those stairs. I've got bungalow legs," she said.

"Are you all right?"

"Yes. One of the nurses helped me to make this call. Putting money in this phone is like feeding strawberries to a donkey. Are *you* all right?" she asked.

"I'm all right."

"Have you ever had a cold shower?" she asked. "I have one every morning."

"Can you get warm when you come out?" I asked.

"I've got to go now. Bye." "Bye," she said again, her voice echoing down the corridor.

"Bye," I said. "Lots of love."

"Pardon?"

The phone clicked dead.

The week before I visited Mum had posted copies of two black and white photographs to me. She had them made from the originals in the family album. She was in her nurse's uniform – in the first she is standing with an older colleague from Ward 17, in the second she is on her own. Her dress is nipped in at the waist, there are bars on her shoes and her wide smile is framed with billowing curls.

Dad drove us through the village and over the level crossing. The River Irwell was gushing over the weir at the bridge. As we reached the top road I could look back over the rows of stone buildings rooted in the valley and at Holcombe Hill in attendance beyond. The road slipped into Bury then out towards Rochdale. Though I'd been told the hospital had improved it looked much the same.

"It hasn't changed that much, has it?" I said to Dad.

It was the same solid Accrington red brick, cigarette ends around the entrance, and familiar smells in the corridor – stale bodies, drugs and bleach.

Even though she was expecting us Mum looked startled to see us, and she didn't smile. I held her frail body in my arms.

A woman with grey hair, bare gums and a permanent smile stood beside me. We looked at the photographs of the staff together. She pointed at each one.

"That's Philip. That's Vicki. That's Sheila."

Mum beckoned to me. We took the lift down two floors. I tucked her hair back into its pleat. The clasp on her combs jutted out beyond her hair, but she wasn't bothered.

"It's my aerial," she said.

On the ground floor the lift doors opened onto a hallway and an office with floral curtains around the windows.

"That's where they gave me my buffet when I was going to get married."

I remembered her pointing out the room when she was first admitted. As we walked past the lawns I also remembered the black and white photographs Mum had sent which must have been taken there forty years before.

Mum wanted us to eat in the Broad Oak Suite – the hospital restaurant.

"It's very reasonable. Upmarket, " she said.

I'd heard a lot about the Broad Oak Suite over the last few months. How she'd go there with a fellow patient and have a meal. Soup and a roll, a sweet, coffee on the veranda. That way she could choose what she ate, she didn't have to fill in a menu card, and she didn't have to eat at a table off a plastic tablecloth with the other patients.

After we'd eaten the three of us sat in the car. Starlings scratched about the tarmac. The clouds lifted high enough for a slit of sunlight to push through. Mum's voice was soft and gentle – it came from deep within her; it had mostly lost the edge she used to keep the world at bay when she was unwell. She talked about the patients.

"Gladys. She's a sad case. I don't know why she's in there. She doesn't seem too bad to me. Her husband had a stroke. She wore herself out looking after him. She's as far through as a tram ticket. They wanted her to go in a nursing home. But her husband's already in a nursing home and they would have had to pay for it. So she was put on Ward 17."

"For a rest?" asked Dad.

"Yes, for a rest," said Mum.

"Do the nurse's wear uniforms at night?" I asked.

"Yes. In case there's an emergency. Then they know who's staff and who's a patient."

"You seem a bit better, love," said Dad.

"I want to go to a convent in Spain or Italy and bake cakes," said Mum.

I visited again when she was back home. She was pale with dark circles around her eyes – eyes alert with medication. She walked purposefully around the bungalow without purpose. She held her hands out in front of her with a pleading look.

"I know what I want for my old age," she said that afternoon. "An Abbeyfield Home. You can take your own piece of furniture. You have breakfast on your own and the other meals communally. £200 a week. I've got it all worked out. You don't need to worry."

The yellow flag iris were standing tall in the front garden while the heads of montbretia swayed in the breeze. Each evening Mum put the used teabags around the pot plants and tubs outside. The wind blew them across the lawn. It came time for me to leave.

"Where's Mum?" I asked.

"She's in her room," said Dad. "In tears."

"Why?"

"Why do you think?"

Mum appeared, bleary eyed.

"Drive carefully," she said. "Ring me when you get back."

"I will."

"I'll stand at the window."

Dad followed me out to my car.

"Do you have to go?" he said.

"Yes, Dad, I do."

"Why? I need you here."

"I have to live my life."

"Is that it?"

We stood for a minute and looked at each other before I unlocked my car. I started the engine and reversed up the drive. When I looked back Dad was waving from the end of the garden and Mum was waving from the shadows of the living room.

When I spoke to Mum the following week I asked her how she was feeling.

"I'm coping. I always cope. Live for the day. You never know what's around the corner. I've had a lot of corners in my life. Live for the day and have a dream."

14 Piercings

As I washed up, Mum sat behind me in her usual chair. Her breathing was heavy. She had her puffer in one hand and a cigarette in the other. Underneath the table was a scatter of brown criss-cross burns where she'd dropped her cigarettes on the lino. The lino had been replaced twice.

"That knob's not pressed in," said Mum.

She didn't like it if all the knobs on her new caramel cooker were not flush with the fascia. I pressed in the recalcitrant knob.

"Are you going to dry them?" she asked.

"I don't usually. I'm a great believer in evaporation."

"You and your London ways." I picked up the blue check tea towel.

"The bin's crooked," she said. It was slightly tipped up on the plant stand. I put it back square on the floor.

"Have you got your medication sorted?" I asked. I was never quite sure what she took when.

"Yes. This egg cup's for dinner, this one for tea."

"How's your pain?"

"Not too bad today."

"Do you need any paracetamol?"

"No, I'll do without."

There weren't many paracetamol left in the cupboard. Mum's main carer had removed most of them the week before. While Mum was in the bathroom the carer told me that they weren't allowed to leave quantities of paracetamol in their clients' houses any more. One carer had gone round from house to house collecting the lot. Her suicide attempt had been successful.

Through the window I could see rooftops staggering down

to the village and the four sturdy pinnacles of St Andrew's Church. Up on the right Emmanuel Church emerged from the trees on the lower slopes of Holcombe Hill. It wasn't a bad place to have visited since I left home.

"The kettle's not straight," said Mum. I put it back on its base.

"I've never found that money," she said.

"How much was it?"

"Four hundred pounds."

"I've asked the decorator. He reckons his boys are completely trustworthy."

"Then I don't know what to think."

I didn't like to think of Mum being prey to any workman who wanted to rip her off. I blazed when she told me that a man from the village had charged her ten pounds to come up and change a light bulb; but she wouldn't let me speak to him. What would she do if she needed another light bulb changing? We'd looked all over the bungalow for the money. She'd put it away somewhere when she knew the decorators were due. Every drawer and cupboard had been scoured.

"Do you fancy going on holiday?" I asked.

"Where to?"

"I've found this hotel in Wales. It caters for the disabled. They have all the equipment. And they have carers to get you up and give you a bath. You can have your hair done... there's even a swimming pool."

"I'll not be swimming."

"No, I know. What do you think?"

"When would we go?"

"I was thinking April, for a week. Over the Easter weekend."

"How much is it?"

"It's not that expensive."

"I can't remember when I last had a holiday. We used to go everywhere. Magaluf, Dunoon, Arc de Triomphe..."

"You took us on some great holidays, Mum. What was it Warren's teacher said? 'He's been taken about to interesting places'? I thought everyone was! I came across a Year 3 child last week who's never seen the sea. Ruksar."

"Is that his name?"

"Her. Yes."

"Dad'll not go on another holiday."

"No. I know."

"I couldn't visit him last week. My pain was too bad."

"We'll go tomorrow." .

"How would we get to Wales?"

"I'll drive. I'll come up and we can set off from here. I'll go and find the brochure."

I walked past Dad's bedroom. His vascular dementia meant he now lived in a home. At first Mum thought he would come back to live at the bungalow again, but she now accepted that he wouldn't. Dad's chest of drawers was piled high with towers and pyramids of tins: potatoes, peaches, marrowfat peas, frankfurters, butter beans, soup, condensed milk, rice pudding and corned beef. There were boxes of sugar-free jelly, jars of coffee and jars of sugar-free sugar. Mum called it 'the shop.' I arranged the tins for her when I found twenty-one large tins of potatoes in plastic bags on the floor, along with numerous other tins. The carers didn't have time to check what she needed and Mum would re-order every week. With the shop she could see what she'd got. I found the brochure in the big bedroom where I slept.

"Look, Mum, 'the Philip Roe Resort Hotel has developed an outstanding reputation for its warm welcome, fine service and excellent cuisine. Double, twin, single and family rooms available…'"

"We could have two singles."

"Well we both snore!" She picked out a paragraph. "'Choice of bath or wheel-in shower, electrical adjustable beds, emergency call points …' I can take my red button with me."

"You won't need that. It won't work down there. They won't come down to Wales to pick you up off the floor!"

"I'm not taking it off. Or else I'll be looking for that biscuit under the settee."

"Like Thora Hird? With the cream cracker?"

"Whatever it was."

'Oh well,' I thought, 'what does it matter whether she wears her emergency button or not? At least she presses it now and doesn't stay on the floor all night not wanting to disturb anyone like she did when she first got it.' I continued reading from the brochure.

" 'The Rafters Restaurant is renowned for its mouth-watering menus using only fresh local ingredients.' "

"You'd better get the suitcases down. And we'd better make some money. Put the pan on and get out the bottle tops!"

The drive was long and uncomfortable for my mother. She didn't often complain so when she did I knew her arthritis was particularly bad. We finally arrived at Cowbridge and the hotel – a low-level brick building with flowerbeds to the front and a huge pond at the back. It almost avoided looking like an institution, but not quite. That evening, when we'd unpacked in our separate rooms and Mum was tucked up in bed in her nightie with a mug of tea, my shoulders relaxed. A relieved wave of tears washed through me.

Next morning I wheeled Mum to the dining room for breakfast. We were competing with other residents in motorized wheelchairs.

"They look good," said Mum, as they spun themselves round and zipped up and down the corridors. "Perhaps Father Christmas will be good to me."

"Well that would make a change. When I ask you what you want you usually say three hankies."

I slotted her chair under a vacant table.

"What would you like to do today?" I asked.

"Shall we go and look at the shops?"

"If you like."

I knew she wanted new earrings for her Golden Wedding.

It was the beginning of April and the anniversary was in May. We stopped at every jewellers the length and breadth of Cowbridge High Street. An assistant at the most exclusive shop saw us peering in the window and unlocked the door. I tipped Mum's wheelchair up over the step and pushed her into the womb of the shop.

"Are you looking for clip-ons or pierced?"

Mum touched her right ear lobe.

"Clip-ons," she said.

Nestled on a red velvet pad were a pair in white gold with diamonds, and a pearl tucked into a central swirl.

"Those are nice," said Mum, pointing. The assistant took them out of the case and handed them to Mum one by one.

"The mirror's over there," she said, showing her an oval framed with bronze curlicues. Mum turned her head from side to side admiring the jewels sparkling in her ears.

"How much are they?"

"Four hundred and seventy five pounds."

I looked at Mum, aghast. She rooted in her handbag.

"Is my card out of date?" she asked, thrusting her cash card at me.

"No," I said. "Shall we have a think about it? We could go and have a coffee?"

Back on the pavement we both laughed.

"You weren't going to buy those were you?"

"I was tempted."

In the midst of a garden centre, next to pools of Malaysian Koi Carp and Comet Goldfish, we sat with steaming Horlicks mugs of coffee.

"I want to wear all my finery for the golden wedding, but it's all in the drawer under my bed."

"What's in there?"

"My gold bracelet, my locket… all kinds of things."

"Will it not open?"

"I hope so. But that side of the bed is pushed up against the wall."

"I can get in it for you."

"Yes." She paused. "If I have gold earrings they won't give me an infection."

"Are your ears still pierced?"

"I've had them pierced twice, but they've closed up. And look at this." She showed me her ear – it was split across the lobe.

"We can try and get them pierced when we go to Porthcawl," I suggested.

"I think that would be wise. I don't want to pay a lot for earrings for them to just fall off."

"You could have them as your present."

Despite the chilly breeze buffeting the promenade at Porthcawl we sat with a curl of ice cream each and watched the glittering sea. Mum's cornet spread around her mouth like mine did when I was a child.

We continued the investigation of jewellers, this time for piercing opportunities. I left Mum outside the shops while I popped in quickly to ask if they did it. When I said Mum's ears had already been pierced they weren't interested. Two assistants refused outright and a third came out to see Mum but shook her head when she saw Mum's split ear.

At the end of the high street was a hairdresser's painted electric blue and playing reggae music. They advertised piercing on a sparkly notice in the window. A young woman with a very black ponytail and six silver rings up the side of each ear came out to have a look.

"No problem. Come in. I can do it straight away."

She swabbed Mum's ears, took her piercing gun and pointed at a plump part of Mum's lobe. Two clicks, two studs, advice on aftercare and we were done.

We fell into a routine of visits and meals and drinks and drives; the Brecon Mountain Railway where the guard sang to us in the wheelchair and bicycle carriage as we passed a drowned parish in the Pontsticill Reservoir; the National Botanic Garden where Mum announced to a man doing a questionnaire that we were staying in 'the disabled hotel;' the soft sandy domes of the Brecon Beacons whose contours overwhelmed us as we sat at their base.

When I drove back to the hotel Mum was invariably asleep.

"Mum, you're missing all this lovely countryside."

"I'm just trying to get used to going round these corners."

On Easter Monday, our penultimate day, we made for Penarth, stopping at Barry Island Tourist Office on the way. It was closed for lunch. A man banged on my window.

"Don't stop there. There's a traffic warden across the road. She's a witch. She'll book you at any opportunity." I thanked him and we drove on.

"How are you ears now?" I asked Mum.

"I've been twisting the studs."

"Like the hippy chick said?"

"Yes." She laughed. "One of the nurses ripped an earring out of my ear when I tried to escape. That's why it split."

"Did she mean to do it?"

"I don't think she did. I was running across the room and she grabbed my ears and pulled them."

I remembered not knowing who to believe – my Mum who was distressed with her ear caked in blood, or the nurse whose excuse was that Mum kept running away. Now, thirty years later, this score was settled.

"I escaped once with all my stuff in a pillowcase. It was snowing outside and I went across the road to the Wagon and Horses. Ron Greenhalgh ran it. I'd known him for years. He took me to his house and rang the nurse to bring me back."

Traffic lights and pedestrians were behaving as they usually did. What Mum was saying was a revelation to me. All those times she'd been ill we just got through it, and never referred to it afterwards.

"They were tough years. Did I tell you about the rose?"

"No, I don't think you did."

"They had a rose garden laid out in front. I saw this beautiful rose. I picked it and wrapped it in a bit of paper. When I went to see Dr Ball I gave it to him."

Dr Ball was Mum's long serving, ineffectual, it seemed to me, psychiatrist.

"They had this flat roof. I said it would be ideal for a swimming pool."

"I bet they loved you."

"They've got the same stairs they had when I was working there. There was one nurse who came on night shift with a valise, her knitting, and jam butties for the ones who couldn't sleep."

We stopped at traffic lights.

"Dad would phone me on the ward to ask me out. Our first date on our own was on Christmas Eve. He gave me a pair of pearl earrings. I hadn't bought him anything – I didn't know he was going to give me a present. But I've got him something every year since."

We pulled away.

"The ECT was very frightening. You didn't get dressed and you didn't have any breakfast. You lay down and they put clamps on your head. Then you shook."

"You always looked very pale afterwards."

"I can't say it did any good. And you lose parts of your memory."

Now I could ask the question I'd never been able to ask before. As I got older I became more involved when Mum was admitted to Ward 17. I'd be called away from London by my Auntie Betty to come and help my father. I'd be resentful at first, not wanting to be pulled away from my own life. Betty would tell me that Dad needed me. He became baffled and beaten when Mum was ill. I would persuade her as gently as I could that Ward 17 was the best place for her to be. It was what she feared the most. I'd pack her things and Dad would drive us to the hospital. On one occasion, as I sat in on her interview at the back of the ward office, Mum was asked a series of routine questions. Had she ever attempted suicide? Her answer was 'Yes.' At first I disbelieved what I heard. Then, when I travelled home on the train I stared out of the window trying to imagine how she must have felt to want to do that. She made another attempt several years later. My Dad came home and found her on the living room floor with a bottle of whisky and a bottle of pills by her side.

"Did you mean to kill yourself when you tried?"

"Yes I did. But I'm glad now I didn't."

The sun lit a strip of sea the length of the horizon.

"I pray every night. For you – good work and safe driving; for your brother – not to work too hard; for the children – good school work; for me – to keep well. I tend to forget Dad now."

Rain began to fall in fine veils. The wipers squeaked across the windscreen. Mum fell asleep. We never reached Penarth.

The next day Mum had her hair done and I took photographs of her next to the large pond. In one shot she's throwing her arms back over her head, pretending to fall back into the pond.

I helped her pack. We laid her clothes in piles on the bed. I unzipped her suitcase and prised open its jaws. After layering the clothes in the bottom of the case I slipped my hand into the silky pocket in the lid.

"What's in here?" I asked.

My fingers stubbed against a wedge of notes. Four hundred pounds in tens and fivers.

"That's where it was!" said Mum.

She talked about our holiday for weeks.

The New Year had started. I wanted to smash the china and glass display at Alder's sale; the Croydon branch was dense with discounts and offers. Pyramids of bulging red wineglasses and ladders of flutes were asking for it. There was a particularly cocky arrangement of Royal Doulton seconds – fine white china with gold rims, which definitely had it coming.

It wasn't as if Christmas had been an out and out disaster. The day had begun with Jacques Loussier playing Bach, and a little snow – a fine flurry settling on the night's frost. I sorted through the albums in my parents' radiogram – James Last and his Orchestra, Herb Alpert and his Tijuana Brass, Kiri te Kanawa. I stacked up likely contenders to play through the day.

I had driven up from London the day before. The traffic had been surprisingly light but the journey took six hours. When I hit Ramsbottom the Victorian Fayre was putting away its stalls. The Christmas lights over the shops were delicate and fleeting, unlike the clumsy lumpen lights I'd left behind in Lewisham.

The bungalow looked the same as ever – solid and snug, like a familiar illustration in a children's book. The garden was overgrown – the trees and shrubs were indistinguishable from one another, and the plastic urns were blown over onto their sides. I picked up two bottles of milk from the doorstep and took them in with me. Mum had taken to keeping strange items in the fridge – a packet of sugar, a box of dried lasagne, a bag of boiled sweets. I pulled them out.

"It's damp in the cupboards," said Mum in her defence.

It took a while for me to slot into the mode of my mother's home. The kitchen floor and the bathroom floor were filthy.

"Hasn't your cleaner been?" I asked.

"Sonia? She wouldn't come."

"Why not?"

"She wouldn't come while the decorators were here. She didn't want to clean everything and then…"

"…it all get dirty again." I often finished off Mum's sentences.

The newly papered anaglypta walls undulated with various different designs; but the curtains were rolled up on the beds, and Mum's ornaments, pictures and mirrors were boxed up in the sunroom. Mum called it 'the conservatory.' To me, a conservatory was a splendour of Victorian glass built into a beautiful shape. But my mother was proud of her PVC extension, even if now it did only house dried flowers and a couple of intrepid geraniums. Mum had tried to replace the brass swans and the Dick Turpin toby jug on the shelves by the fireplace, but her arthritis soon sent her into her high-backed chair with a hot water bottle.

When Jacques Loussier finished I put on Moura Lympany playing Chopin waltzes and got out the mop and bucket.

"Do it on Boxing Day," my mother pleaded.

"I'm not having Christmas Day with dirty floors," I said. I couldn't say, 'I'm not having Christmas dinner with dirty floors,' because we were due to go out for our festive meal. We had an invitation, from Hawthorn Clough.

I screwed the grey mop round in the sieve of the orange plastic bucket and dragged it across the kitchen floor. The Chopin was jumping over the scratches on the L.P.. As the piano swelled towards crescendos I swathed the floors with grey water. I stroked and soaked and smoothed the floors until all that was left were the cigarette burn marks under the table. Mum had started to smoke when she was fifteen. At seventy-four she wasn't about to stop. What frightened me was her smoking in the kitchen in middle of the night. What if she dozed off? I said to her that catching fire wouldn't be a good way to go. "You can get me a fire extinguisher!" she said.

I abandoned the mop for the hoover. The sun streamed into the dining room.

"You can see the dust when the sun shines," said Mum. She spoke slowly and deliberately, each word an effort. There were frequent pauses and hesitations.

"Do you want to watch the Queen's speech?" I asked. "If we get back in time."

"I'm out of touch. I'm not bothering. She's off my mailing list. She's had such a horrible year. And all her family... I might watch her speech."

I found a feather duster in the umbrella stand and set about the sideboard, flicking a pathway through the dust on the mahogany surface. Six frosted shot glasses stood next to a Capo di Monte figure who was frying an egg on his bony knee.

Hawthorne Clough is a residential care home in Holcombe Brook. My father had lived there for eight months. We'd been told that if we arrived by eleven forty-five we could eat Christmas dinner with him. I put on my make-up – the same make-up I'd been wearing for fifteen years. Mum put on a pair of lace-up shoes instead of the slippers which she usually wore inside and out, for comfort.

I made a quick phone call. I wanted to hear David's voice. We'd been together for five years. We hadn't wanted to spend Christmas apart, but our parents were at opposite ends of the country. He was attending to his parents in Edenbridge.

"Happy Christmas."

"Happy Christmas David."

"Is it?"

"Too early to say. I'll tell you later."

David's parents were slightly younger, more mobile and more part of the world. They did line dancing, drove a new car and went on holiday to Majorca. I envied them their quality of life on my parents' behalf.

By the time I pushed Mum to the car, the water which I had earlier dribbled over the windscreen had frozen into a rivulet on the path.

"What's that?" asked my mother, pointing. "Is your car leaking?"

When she stood up I could see that her clothes were tangled up in her Tens machine. It was supposed to help relieve her osteoarthritis. The wires made scalloped edges along the bottom of her skirt. As she tucked herself into the passenger seat and I pushed the car door shut the wheelchair wheeled itself back to the front door. As we drove through the village and along the main roads Mum counted burglar alarms.

Hawthorn Clough is an old coaching house – stone walls turned black, and dependable windows. It could've been a scene from a Bronte novel – women moving gracefully in long frocks, horses trotting on wet cobbles. Instead it is a home for the forgotten and forlorn. The cars in the car park mostly belonged to the staff.

Dad was sitting in the lounge – the second lounge, for the badly behaved. Not that they could help it, but the residential home residents wouldn't put up with a continuous loop of shouting, or impromptu urination from the 'mentally infirm'.

"Norman, you've got visitors," said Peter. Peter was a familiar member of staff to my mother and I. He kissed us both for Christmas. It felt slightly uncomfortable. Dad stirred and tried to turn round. His eyes were milky and wet.

"Hello," said Mum brightly, trying to jog him into recognition. Dad grabbed her hand.

"Could we open presents in his room?" I asked Peter.

"Of course." He led the way and unlocked the door of my father's room. He and Mum ambled along the corridor arm in arm.

The bedclothes were bunched up near the top of the bed. The pillows lay side by side on the floor. I raised my hand to my nose and mouth to stifle the smell of urine.

"Shall I open the window?" asked Peter.

"Yes please," I said. Neither of us referred to the smell.

"Sorry we haven't done this room yet. I'll get someone to come. Would you like more chairs?" He wedged the door of the room open and went in search of furniture.

Mum manoeuvred herself into the armchair and heaved a

sigh of relief. Peter returned with two extra chairs. He guided my father so that the back of his legs were touching the seat of the bigger chair.

"Sit down now Norman. Sit down. Bend your legs."

Now that Dad was standing, he was reluctant to abandon himself to sitting. It took a huge leap of faith for him to believe that the chair would be there if he surrendered to it.

"Sit down Norman. That's it." Dad's legs gave way and the chair caught him.

"When I got him up this morning I told him it was Christmas Day. He said, 'I must buy a box of chocolates for my wife.' He's lovely. Aren't you Norman? He's no trouble." Peter tousled my father's hair as though he was six years old. Then he quickly made the bed and left.

My Dad's hair had been cut into an uncharacteristic style. Usually he wore it combed back, neat, off his forehead. Here they combed it forward to look like Frank Sinatra in his later years.

"You've got some cards," said Mum.

I rearranged them on the melamine chest of drawers.

"Who are they from?" There was a hint of jealousy in her voice. This was part of her husband's life she didn't know about.

"This one's from the home," I said, trying to clear up the mystery. "This one's from David and me. The rest are from the family."

"I don't want to lose you," my father said to his wife. "I don't want you to marry someone else." Mum stroked his hand. "It's all right," she said.

"Here's a present for you, Dad." I passed him a golden parcel from my basket. He looked down at it but didn't know what to do. I helped him to pull at the sellotape. He was concerned about damaging the wrapping paper. It was a green cardigan-fleece with a nametape stitched inside the neckline. He opened more presents. A huge bar of his favourite Bourneville chocolate, some green slippers, and a pack of Karate shower gel, soap and deodorant.

"Do you have a shower?" I asked. There wasn't a shower at the bungalow. He didn't answer. I tried again. "Do you have a bath or a shower?" He didn't answer. What he did say was, "You've done me really proud. I'm going to document all this and give it to people less fortunate than myself."

"Oh God!" I said, not meaning to speak out loud.

The day before he left his home for good my father sat with me on the sofa. He'd been a member of the Rossendale Male Voice Choir. We listened together to a tape of him singing, and we sang along to 'Mud Mud Glorious Mud.'

"How do you know this?" he asked. "From school?"

"No. From listening to the tape. You gave me a copy."

"Did I?" he looked into the middle distance then back at me. "You know I'm losing my reason?"

I paused. "Do you mind?"

"Not really. As long as I can keep going."

"What keeps you going?"

"Things that need doing."

"Do you remember the planes you mended in the war? Blenheims and Hurricanes."

"Spitfires and Mosquitoes."

"Multi-Vengeance Dive Bombers." He took my hand, put it on his lap and looked down.

He wandered from room to room less and less able to focus on an activity or a thought; he watered the pan stand instead of the plant stand; he poured milk into the sugar bowl. He came back from the village with four lots of cake having been asked not to buy any. When he got ready for bed he put his vest over his shirt and his pyjamas over his vest. Every few minutes he would go into the kitchen and ask Mum,

"Anything outstanding?"

"He talks to himself now," Mum whispered to me when we were alone.

I began saying and doing things I didn't normally do or say. I would kiss his forehead and hold his hand; I would say,

"Take Care" and "God Bless" when I left him.

But the next day he tripped on the uneven flags around the bungalow. He fell and cracked a rib. After six weeks in hospital he had deteriorated so much that returning home was out of the question. The staff at Hawthorn Clough tried to reassure me that he was reasonably happy.

Peter popped his head round the door.

"Would you like to eat in here? We could set up a table. It'd be no trouble."

"Oh yes please," said Mum. "You can have the top off my egg any day."

I was relieved. At least we would have some privacy. I hadn't relished the thought of eating in the second lounge with the other residents. A procession of trolleys, tablecloths, crackers and cutlery arrived. Peter laid the table, rearranged the chairs and placed plastic glasses next to red napkins. Then he closed the window. While we waited for the food I pulled a cracker with Dad.

"Pull. Pull hard," I reminded him. He put on his yellow crown and I read out the joke.

"Why did the boy put his granddad in the fridge?" No one offered an answer. "Because he fancied an ice cold pop."

One of the housekeepers appeared at the door holding a bundle of clean clothes.

"Do you mind if I put these in Norman's chest of drawers."

"No," said Mum and I in unison.

She placed the clothes in neat piles in two of the drawers and smoothed them over.

"I'll just close that window," she said. She fastened the handle, smiled, and left.

Dad drained his wine as though it were lemonade. When the food arrived it did its best to avoid his knife and fork. Sprouts tumbled off his plate; an angel on horseback fell to the floor. He put down his knife and fork and lifted a thin slice of turkey to his mouth.

"Not with your hands," I said sharply. I couldn't bear to see the last traces of civilized behaviour slip away from him.

"No, Daughter," he said. I took a spoon and began to feed him.

By twelve forty five we had finished our meal. I opened the window. The fields stretched away to the foothills of the Pennines. Holcombe Hill rose on the horizon with its sturdy stone tower. Dad and I had walked up that hill, down it, along it and beside it. He could still see the tower. I didn't know if that was a comfort to him or a torment.

"I rather like my family," he said. "But I hated their guts when they started to move away. It's chaos in here. Routine, routine, routine. Get you up in the morning, put you to bed at night. Breakfast, dinner and tea. Breakfast, dinner and tea." He turned to my mother. "You don't come very often!" Mum bowed her head and looked down at her lap.

I felt for them both. My father spent large tracts of time away from those he loved. My mother, who had lived with her husband for forty-eight years now saw him only once a week, if she was well enough. Dad didn't understand how Mum struggled through each week, besieged by the home helps, the district nurse, the chiropodist, the physio; if it wasn't the hairdresser at the door, it was the cleaner, the gardener, the Teleshop food delivery or the travelling librarian.

He talked on, making less and less sense. "I think about getting a carrot off the floor. We could do with a bit of hardboard between here and knitwear." Finally he got up and wandered into the lounge, first making sure that he had a pocketful of chocolate. Mum and I followed and sat beside him on the quadrangle of chairs. A woman was having an argument with the Christmas tree. Three ladies sat looking very serious in winged armchairs, each with a black eye. A young girl ate scraps off the tablecloth and the floor, then tried to eat a small glass tree in a pot.

Dad turned to me and said, "I must keep in touch with the outside world. What is your address? What is your phone number?"

By the time we left he'd nodded off.

That evening, after a long dose of television and two glasses of advocaat Mum said, "Thank-you for making Christmas vulnerable." She paused. "Bearable I should say."

When I visited my father on my own on Boxing Day I asked him what had happened the day before.

"We didn't have turkey," he said.

"Did you get any presents?"

"Bits of things. From China. My family came."

I picked up a pack of six substantial tumblers and took them to the checkout. I wanted glasses which wouldn't break easily. The assistant packed them carefully in tissue and dropped them into a large carrier. I found my car in the multi-storey and headed north. It was dusk. The light was slipping between gentian and Prussian blue. I turned off the main drag to a piece of derelict land. One wall remained from a bulldozed row of houses. I parked the car so that it faced the wall and left the lights on. I took the carrier, stood in front of the car, and one by one hurled the glasses at the wall. Each time I threw harder and aimed higher so I could see the glass skitter. The crashes were loud and satisfying. I stood for a minute then drove home, with little respect for the speed limit.

The house was dark but David was home – I had seen his car parked outside. I climbed the stairs and peeped into the bedroom. He was lying on top of the duvet; his eyes were closed, his breathing deep. I lay down next to him and unbuttoned the top buttons of his shirt. My fingers threaded themselves through the thick hair on his chest. His skin warmed my hand.

16   Dream of Me

As I turned into the driveway I noticed that 'Hawthorne' was carved into the stone pillar on the left, but 'Clough' on the right was obliterated by ivy. I pulled up in the car park. Holcombe Tower still stood reassuringly on the clear horizon. A smattering of snowdrops glowed from corners of the flowerbeds. I pressed the doorbell, pushed the front door open, and waved at the manager who was speaking on the phone as I passed her office.

In the nursing home dining area a man was sat at one of the tables. He moved the salt and pepper and sugar bowl to the centre of the tablecloth, then moved them to the edge; to the centre, to the edge – always in the same combination and in the same position.

"Norman was in his room the last time I saw him," said Joanna, one of the staff, who was sitting at another table sorting out a board game. "He's had Jaffa cakes and chocolate for breakfast. And I've got to tell you - he came up to me yesterday and said, 'Where's the main switch?' I said 'What do you want with a main switch? I don't know of any main switch.' 'You're no use to me,' he said, and walked away, laughing his head off."

I smiled. The name of the board game was written in yellow letters on the lid – FRUSTRATION.

There were two ladies walking arm in arm up and down the corridor wearing matching turquoise cardigans. The taller one stopped me.

"We're doing a bit of study. Can you give us any advice?" I pointed to where the lounge was. She seemed happy enough.

The door to Dad's room was open. He was sitting in his winged armchair gazing towards the window, wearing his own shirt and someone else's jogging bottoms.

"Hiya," I said.

His face broke into a smile. I bent down and put my arm around his shoulders and kissed his smooth cheek.

"Eh Darlin'," he said.

"I've brought you a geranium, Dad. I grew it from a cutting. It's called 'First Love.'

"I hope I'm not your last," he said.

I put the plant on the windowsill, hoping someone would water it. The flowers were white with a flush of salmon pink in the centre.

Dad stuck his tongue out. "I want a drink of orange."

Then he asked, "What's wrong with me?" I stood beside him and smoothed his hair.

He looked thin but I knew he ate well. It was his endless wandering up and down the corridors which consumed his energy. Apparently every few months all the patients stood up and made a bid for freedom by heading for the front door.

"I've been in here eight days and haven't had a decent conversation," said Dad.

I pulled up the upright chair, put his hand in mine and ran my fingers over the parallel ridges along his fingernails.

"*We* can talk," I said.

"Nice shoes,"

"Thanks, Dad."

"Secrete your watch under your pillow."

"OK."

"I miss you," he said.

"I miss you too."

"Sorry for the worry."

"Don't worry."

"You'll go and you'll come back."

"I will."

"It's chaos in here. I mean that. It'll make a good write-up."

Just then Joanna appeared at the door with a tray of tea and biscuits.

"I'll just put them down here." She placed the tray on the

bed and left. I handed Dad the plate of biscuits. He went straight for the jammy dodger and the custard cream and ate them with gusto.

"No joy, no pleasure, no holidays. Trapped," he said. This cut me to the quick. "What is the prognosis of my life?"

"I don't know, Dad." I held his hand again.

"Does your television protrude?" he asked. I edged closer to him. "This is how it should be," he said. "I want you to be happy."

He looked ever more frail with creamy eyes, fleecy hair and cramped hands. He had a biscuit crumb on his bottom lip. He licked it into his mouth.

"Like a lizard," I said. At the same time he said, "Iguana." We laughed.

"Dad, I've got some news. Some not very good news." Alarm shot through his eyes.

"It's Mum. She's really not well. She's in hospital. It's her chest." He looked bewildered.

"I hate myself," he said, looking at the carpet.

I poured the tea and splashed it into the saucers and onto the tray.

"Oh dear," we both said.

"Will they let me in?" he asked.

"We could take you to see her. I'm sure we could do that." He looked a bit brighter.

"Mum is a choc-alcoholic."

At twelve thirty we ambled to the communal room where dinner was underway. Plastic aprons had been tied round the patients' necks and food was being served from the trolley. Those who couldn't manage to feed themselves were being fed. Joanna was standing in the doorway.

"He likes the lounge," she said to me. "And his little brain likes to wander up and down the corridor." She took Dad's hand.

"Are you ready for your dinner, Norman?" she asked. Then she looked at me. "It's like feeding time at the zoo in here," she said.

We sat Dad down in a comfortable chair.

"My earsight isn't very good," he said.

"Say goodbye," said Joanna.

He kissed her instead of me. I touched his cheek and waved as I walked away.

"I need you," he called after me. "Please, please, please..." His voice echoed down the corridor.

As I passed the manager's office on the way out I hovered and agonized over whether to question Joanna's 'zoo' comment with her. I felt like a parent who didn't want to cause any upset for her child in primary school. I knew this was the best place in the area for Dad, and that in a few days I'd be hundreds of miles away. I buzzed for the front door to be opened and waved goodbye.

Hawthorne Clough loaned a member of staff to accompany Dad to the hospital. Lee had known Dad for a while and they liked each other. He put his hand on top of Dad's head to make sure he cleared the car door frame.

"This has changed," said Dad as we drove through Bury Bridge.

"They're building new shops, Norman," said Lee. "We've got a Carphone Warehouse now."

We guided Dad into the lift at the hospital and introduced ourselves at the reception on Ward 6 – Cardiorespiratory.

"Mary's just along there – third bed down," said the nurse.

As Dad approached Mum's bed he put his arms out. Mum's eyes widened as she saw him coming towards her. Dad took her hands in his.

"You're mine," he said. They smiled at each other.

"I'm so pleased to see you," said Dad.

"I'm so pleased to see *you*," said Mum.

Lee and I sat Dad down then we hung back in the doorway.

They touched each other's faces and Dad ran his thumb across Mum's wedding and eternity rings. They gazed steadily into each other's eyes.

"Dream of me in your nice room?" said Mum.

"Pardon?" asked Dad.

"Dream of me in your nice room?"

"Yes I have a nice room. A very nice room."

Mum tired easily and after another few minutes she said gently, "Are you going to make your way now?" I went across and put my hand on Dad's shoulder.

"Dad, we should go now," I said.

"Oh," he said, bending down to kiss his wife.

"Night night," he said.

"Sleep tight," said Mum.

As we drove back to Hawthorne Clough we listened to Glen Gould's thrilling trills and aplomb as he played the Goldberg Variations. Lee and I pointed out the sunset to Dad. The sky blended sugar pink with China blue.

Lee opened the heavy front door.

"Hello, girls," said Dad, over and over.

When I got back to the bungalow I opened the kitchen door onto the garden and made a pot of tea. The Yucca plant pointed to the darkness, and orange pinholes of light shimmered across the valley. That night I dreamt that Dad came home for the weekend. We lived in a caravan. He smiled a lot and drank tea. He was the man he used to be.

The last phone conversation I had with my mother was on a Tuesday in early January from inside a coin box in Burnham Deepdale. Pink-footed geese were flying in convoy high in the sky.

"What are you up to?" I asked.

"I'm having a break."

"What, another one?" I said. She laughed.

"I had the chiropodist round this morning. She said, 'You've had some sad moments in your life. What with ulcers, bunions and damaged toes!"

"Oh Lord! Did she make you more comfortable?"

"Yes."

"Do you still get some pleasure from life Mum?"

"Coronation Street."

"Anything else?"

"I get pleasure from my new duvet. I sleep much better. It's feather. Warren bought it."

"Oh good."

"The chiropodist was slightly coloured."

"You can't say that Mum."

"Why not? What should I say?"

"Mixed race."

"Oh I'm O.F."

"What's that?"

"Old fashioned."

"As long as you're not P.C."

"What's that?"

At Christmas Mum hadn't had much to say. She concentrated on opening her presents and eating. No sooner had she finished one course than she was ready for the next. We had to put restraints on the bottle of advocaat.

At Christmas dinner her false teeth went missing. They weren't comfortable for her so she took them out to eat. After the meal she could find the bottom set but not the top. A search was mounted – over the table, under the table, on her lap... . She found them among the tissues stuffed down her cleavage. Two of her carers had nicknamed her 'The Tissue Queen' because whenever they took off her clothes to get her ready for bed there was always a shower of tissues.

On Boxing Day evening Mum commented on the festivities as she pushed her zimmer frame down the hall to her room.

"Very good," she said, emphatically.

On the Thursday I walked along Brancaster beach. The horizon dissolved into mist. The stretch of ochre sand was broken with razor-shell swirls. Oystercatchers dipped in and out of a channel where it met the sea. The sand was imprinted with the memory of waves.

On my way back to the cottage I was renting I stepped into the village telephone box and called my home number. My answer machine was besieged with messages. Mum was in Fairfield Hospital.

You think you know what a day will bring – a choice of meal with a favourite vegetable, a familiar piece of music, an encounter with a friend... I abandoned the cottage and by late afternoon I'd driven across five counties. I made two calls to the hospital on the way. All the nurse would say in the first call was that Mum was 'very poorly'. Only in retrospect could I translate this euphemism. When I tried to make the second call in Rutland the telephone box ate the last of my change. I went into the petrol station beside and explained. In a rich drop of kindness the attendant offered to let me use her phone.

"The same thing happened to me two weeks ago," she said. I found it unnerving but comforting that someone else had gone through this.

Mum was in a room of her own. She was conscious and could answer my questions. My brother had arrived before me. We sat side by side next to the bed. I held Warren's hand and he held my mother's hand.

"I don't want her to die," I said. "I know she has to. But she's my best friend."

A nurse came in to check on her. She had a swinging ponytail and bold make-up.

"She's not in pain," she said.

When she left I stroked Mum's forehead.

"Are you in pain?" I asked.

"Yes."

When the nurse came back she increased the rate of the morphine driver.

My brother, who can sleep anywhere, bedded down in the ensuite bathroom. I kept vigil through the night, watching Mum's breathing and taking in the arch of her brow and the curve of her cheek.

I wasn't with Mum when she died. By 3.30 the next afternoon I needed to sleep and I went back to the bungalow. By then she was unreachable. Warren called me when she began to slip away but I was too drowsy to drive safely. He took a shower to be ready for the night and when he came out Mum's breathing had stopped.

At midnight I heard Warren's car arrive in the drive. I opened the front door for him and we held each other for a long time in the hallway.

"She died at eleven o'clock," he said as I poured two glasses of whisky. We sat in the kitchen. The central heating chugged into action.

"She would have had tears of joy in her eyes when I was born," said Warren. "I'm glad I was there to cry tears of sorrow when she died."

The next day Warren and I looked at the entries on the carers' sheet. Tuesday, when I'd called her, had been her last good day. On the Wednesday she'd had bananas and milk for breakfast, she ate very little soup at lunchtime, and her jelly was untouched at teatime. The last entry said 'Ambulance and G.P. here. G.P. says Mary quite poorly. Checked fires off and kettle unplugged. Will secure house on leaving'.

I went round each room in the bungalow photographing as I went along. I knew that it would never look quite the same again. I photographed Mum's bedside table with her owl reading glasses, two alarm clocks and her bottle of Oil of Olay lying on its side. I photographed her collections of porcelain thimbles displayed in two wooden cases. I photographed her last zimmer frame and the mantelpiece with its line of family photographs arranged along its length. And finally I photographed her dressing table, where the lid on her pot of jewellery was slightly askew, and where she kept a jar of shell guest soaps and three covered coat hangers decorated with curtains of lace.

Mum would have been lost without Dad. Warren and I drove up to Hawthorne Clough on the Saturday. The soft hills looked welcoming in the thin sunlight. Dad greeted us with a smile, then his face dropped when he saw ours. Warren held his hands as we told him what had happened. I put my head on his shoulder and wept; he comforted me. Then he put his head on my shoulder and I comforted him.

"She's our guardian angel now. She's up there looking out for us," he said. "Thank you for being with her. And for all you've both done."

A wood pigeon came to land on the branch of an ash tree outside the window.

"You've a lot of responsibility on your shoulders," he said.

On the Monday I registered Mum's death at Bury Town Hall. It costs three pounds fifty to be born, and three pounds fifty to die.

On the day of the funeral a milky curtain of mist hung over Holcombe Hill. I'd never seen it so low. The funeral director explained that we would have to drive the long way round to Emmanuel Church to avoid the steep incline on The Rake.

"We can't risk the coffin slipping out of the back door," he said.

Two of the three hearses turned left from Spring Wood Street onto the main road down to the village. A car coming down the hill didn't wait for the third hearse to turn and broke our cortege.

While everyone congregated outside the church the funeral director came over to me. Mum and her coffin had been placed on a long metal extending trolley.

"We're two men down because of the flu. Would you mind if we didn't carry the coffin down the aisle?"

Mum was pushed up the path on the trolley. Snatches of snowdrops were huddling between the gravestones. Dad sat in his wheelchair in the aisle next to our pew. As I took his hand the verger thought to bring him a prayer book. He was quiet all the way through the service. Glynis, Mum's main carer, sat at the back of the church. I wanted to invite her to come back to the bungalow afterwards, but before I could she disappeared down The Rake.

"She's very upset," said one of the other carers.

For a while, when we got back to the bungalow, Dad's head was bowed. Then he brightened up – he knew where he was and he enjoyed the company.

"It was very sudden," he said, when we took him back to Hawthorne Clough.

"I don't mind being in here."

The next day the curtain of mist peeled back to Holcombe Tower.

By the time I returned to Ramsbottom for the funeral I'd decided not to visit Mum in the Chapel of Rest. I wanted to remember her as she was. Janice, at the Funeral Director's did ask me if I wanted to see her. When I said 'No,' she said, "I think that's very wise. She doesn't look as well as she did last Friday." But for a while I didn't quite believe she was dead. And I didn't like to think of her lying in her cold grave.

My guy ropes were frayed. A couple of weeks after the funeral, while I was standing on the Jubilee Line platform waiting for a train, there were a series of announcements.

'The delay is due to someone on the track.'

A few minutes later: 'The delay is due to someone on the train.'

And finally: 'The delay is due to passenger action.'

"Just tell us if they've killed themselves or not!" I shouted.

Inwardly I asked, 'Will someone please teach me how to grieve, and stop me shouting on station platforms?'

'Mind the Doors' came another announcement. I repeated it out loud like a child learning a new language.

Where should I find my mother now? In the long cream kid gloves I retrieved from the ottoman? In the beaded black V-necked top she wore for her fiftieth wedding anniversary when she welcomed friends and family to her home? As I pulled the seeded stems of forget-me-nots from my mother's grave, forget-me-nots which had hung in a shimmer of electric blue visible from the gate of the cemetery, I didn't know what to think.

The archaeological dig through the house was coming to an end. I'd bagged and boxed underwear, ornaments, coats, dresses, books and bath salts. I was down to the surfaces of the furniture, the bottoms of drawers, the back of the sideboard. I'd distributed the fabric of my mother's life amongst the three charity shops in the village. The bags and boxes had been gratefully received. I had yet to see the stippled blue goose or the black glass vase gracing one of their window displays.

I went to visit the house where my mother was born – a three storey blackened terrace in Heap Bridge. While I stood at the back of the house rose bay willow herb rustled in the breeze; the seed heads curved from the stems releasing sugar stealers to the wind. I looked up at the top window. There was my grandfather who I'd never known – his chest packed with brown paper against the cold. He is pointing at an incubator. My mother peeps inside it and coos. Her father carefully cups his hands around a day-old chick and holds it over my mother's hands. Its feet scratch her palm, its down tickles her fingers. She murmurs with delight.

I went across the road to the house where my mother grew up – a red brick terrace. I scrutinized the front – its brown front door, its plain solid window frames. I counted the houses along the terrace so that I could locate the same house from the back. Behind the terrace a path opened onto a stretch of rough grass; the backs of the houses were irregular with varying lengths of extensions, but I easily found the back of my mother's house. There was no longer an outside toilet. No longer a candlelit kitchen.

A snake of schoolchildren walked to the games field at the bottom of the lane. My mother, aged six, peels off and runs round the back of the terrace. She dashes into the yard in front of where I'm standing. Through the window I can see my grandmother, whom I never met, giving my mother a piece of just baked and buttered fly pie. The butter dribbles down her chin. Licking her lips and sliding her fingers up her chin and into her mouth she runs out of the front door and joins her friends. Their mouths water with envy.

Mum has a sore throat. Her Mum puts a sweaty sock round her neck and giggles. She has earache. Her father puts his hanky over the bowl of his pipe and points the stem at her ear.

Mrs Jump lives next door, married to Mr Stamp. They have a radio. My grandfather and Mum's brother, Charlie, start to peel off a patch of wallpaper beside the fireplace. The wallpaper has an apple pattern. The apples have been hung upside-down. They very gently dislodge half a dozen bricks. They can see through to Mrs Jump's front room. Everyone laughs. At five o'clock Mum climbs onto a straight back chair so she can sit next to the hole. It's time for Children's Hour. Then Winterbottom and Murgatroyd:

"What does your watch say?"

"Tick tick."

I see my grandmother, alone, collapsing on the floor. My Auntie Betty, at ten years old, comes home from school and finds her. She runs to the neighbour for help. My grandmother dies in hospital the next day. A cerebral haemorrhage. 'She would never have got better.' Mum is thirteen. Her father buys her and her sister new berets and gabardines for the funeral.

Finally I drove a mile to the house where I was born – a terrace with upended slabs of stone for a garden wall. The day I was born the snow was higher than that wall. The gypsy caravans and cattle were gone from the fields in front. Above the sound of birch trees thrashing in the wind I can hear music – The Nutcracker Suite.

My mother has the radio on in the front room. She is playing with me on the settee – I'm six months old. She is moving my legs in time to the music, telling me I'll have ballet lessons and flit about on stage in a frothy dress. I am chattering with delight.

Older, dressed in a check dress, I am standing in the front garden among the marigolds and lupins. Warren stands next to me with his arm around my shoulders. He wears shorts pulled up to his armpits. He hands me a daisy he has picked from the border.

I returned to my mother's last home. What was left to me were the things she said.

About men: "Don't throw out your dirty washing up water until you know you've got fresh." After I reprimanded her for not wanting to wash herself when she became more and more frail: "I've been up till two o'clock in the morning with that washing machine!"

About managing her affairs: "I want you to have power of eternity."

I locked the front door and unlocked my car. It was piled high with those of my mother's belongings I wanted to keep – a drinks trolley with wide wheels and gold trays, a collection of toast racks, and a huge non-stick paella pan. I'd made a special effort in my own home to make space for these new items. But I'd rather have had my mother.

19   Flowers of the Forest

My father sat bolt upright in his borrowed bed and opened his eyes wider than I'd ever seen them. Then he let out two yelps, like an animal wrenched from a trap. I replied with my own jagged cries, and with that anguished duet he was ripped away. His skin quickly lost its colour, but I carried on stroking his cold hand, and kissing his waxy forehead.

I had visited my father at Hawthorne Clough for the last ten days. When I fed him something he liked he opened his mouth like a bird. If he ate well it felt like a triumph: suet pudding, peas and mash followed by chocolate pudding and green mint custard; cheese pie, beans and mash and two portions of rhubarb crumble and custard. Sometimes he was unresponsive, but then he would turn and look at me as if he'd just woken up.

"It's Christine, your daughter," I said.

"That's nice."

As he became weaker and more distant I simply sat by his bed and wept.

Each day when I left I knew I might receive a call to say he'd got worse, so I kept my mobile switched on day and night. When I arrived the morning he died my battery was flat and the staff found me a charger. I picked up the phone from beneath the bed and called my brother.

"They asked if you were coming up," I explained. "When I said 'No' they asked me to leave the room. They must have sat him up in bed. I came back in the room, and then he died. I think what they did made him die."

"I'll come up tomorrow," said Warren.

It had been hard for him to leave Dad for Bristol and his work the previous weekend, knowing that he would not see his father again.

The staff came in to pay their respects. They were as tactile with him in death as they had been in life. I was grateful for their kind words. Here was the evidence that, despite his dementia, he had meant something to these people – they had loved him in their way, and he them.

The housekeeper came up to me.

"You've lost both your parents now. I want to give you a hug," she said.

When the room emptied I looked round. There was the photograph of Mum in her wheelchair eating an ice cream in Wales; there was another of my parents' fiftieth wedding anniversary, their faces glowing above the candles on the cake. Presents of aftershave, potpourri and face cloths were stacked on the shelves; a large pack of Premier Elite Wipes lay on the windowsill. I sat a while, kissed my father one last time, and drove home to the bungalow.

The only thing Dad had ever mentioned about his funeral was that he wanted a Scottish piper playing 'The Flowers of the Forest'. The funeral directors gave me four phone numbers of pipers. None of them were Scottish. I booked one from Eccles. The others were either out, or weren't suitable. One went into minute-by-minute detail about where he would stand, what he would do and what he would play. The other offered a more expensive package which included playing a quieter set of pipes at the house afterwards.

He said, "You don't want to be tripping over a piper while you're filling your plate with quiche and potato salad."

Two years previously Dad had watched from the hearse as his wife was buried; it had rained incessantly and the ground was too muddy for him to walk to the grave. Now his coffin was being lowered on top of hers. The funeral director had refined the procedure since my mother's burial. Instead of just the vicar throwing soil, the funeral director now approached our family one by one with a shepherdess wicker basket. I reached for a handful of soil from the black mound; there was dandruff on the shoulders of his coat.

Over the last two years the bungalow had stood more or less empty, apart from us staying there to visit my father, and trips up at Christmas and bank holidays, and to the manage the renovation. Anaglypta had been shaved from the walls and replaced with flat planes of 'Lavender Haze,' 'Tealight Cream' and 'Tailwind Blue.' The airing cupboard had been stripped from the bathroom and a pristine white suite installed with an easy-to-manage shower. The Naples yellow kitchen I'd chosen changed over the day from the morning sun streaming through the window to the evening, when theatrical ceiling spots pooled light onto the surfaces. My brother had overseen the rewiring, the rebuilding of the garage and the filling of holes in the roof. He'd bricked up a window in the kitchen to allow for more units, and he'd oiled the beachwood work surfaces three times so that splashes of water stood proud.

At the start of the renovation I arrived at the bungalow after a long drive from London. I opened the front door to a belt of acrid smoke. Warren was up a ladder in the kitchen. There was a small fire beneath him on the dining table.

"What's happened?" I asked. He was holding a blowtorch.

"I'm trying to get this glue off." There were burnt patches across the ceiling where he'd removed the glue which had held the polystyrene tiles. A burning globule had fallen down onto a tea towel on the table.

Now, with only the carpets left to replace, I invited three estate agents round. Would this mean that I could move? Would it mean that my brother could build his extension? The first agent arrived in a curvy silver car wearing a shiny grey suit; his glasses had a thin black bar across the top of each lens. He showed himself round.

"We've done everything bar the carpets," was my opener.

"Nice colours and nice colour changes as you walk through. I would clear the house of furniture, so it's like a show home. People can imagine their own stuff in here. You know – my sofa could go here, my dining table there – kind of thing."

His tone was measured and upbeat.

"And if I were you I'd do the carpets. Everything else is fresh and new and then your eyes go down…. You could get a contract carpet for a thousand pounds – it would add five thousand to the value." He paused. "Biscuit. Keep it neutral." I nodded.

"What price are you looking for?" he said, meeting my gaze."

"What would you say?"

"Two hundred and fifty. You'll struggle to get any higher because of stamp duty. They'll want you to come down, or they'll ask *you* to pay the stamp duty."

"They do that?"

"Oh yes. Or they'll ask you to go halves on it."

"Would you go any higher than two fifty?"

"Two sixty… two seventy five tops."

"Hmmm. Any other advice?"

"Will I offend you if I'm honest?"

"No."

"It's your soft furnishings which let you down. The curtains," he said as he stood in the big bedroom. "Nets are old fashioned." I had washed them for the spring. We walked through into the lounge.

"That blind is really a kitchen blind."

"It was my mum's pride and joy." I remembered her pleasure at picking out the repeating pear and plum fabric.

"Oh well, leave that." He paused. "I do two properties a year."

"Do?"

"Do up, renovate. I love kitchens – granite and stainless steel. We've just got a new one at home."

"Do you cook?" I asked.

"I made a fish dish last week. I like getting everything out and making a mess." He looked out of the front window.

"It's nice to see established trees and shrubs. Is that an acer?"

"Yes," I said. It had been planted to commemorate my niece

who had died aged two and three quarters of congenital heart disease.

"Your generation, your parents' generation – they garden. I'm just getting into it." I had never been referred to before as belonging to a particular generation. When did one generation stop and another start? I didn't see myself as necessarily that much older than this man. Perhaps he'd made an assessment of the generations from the line of family photographs on the mantelpiece.

On the doorstep he turned to me. "I hope this doesn't sound patronising, but you've done sterling work with this renovation. Phone me if you've got any other questions."

An hour later the second agent arrived. His vehicle was a four by four and his suit dark blue.

"I wouldn't bother to change the carpets," he said. "Let them choose their own. Leave some furniture and then organize a van to clear it when it's sold. We've got some phone numbers."

He was altogether more formal than the previous man – older, with rimless spectacles. He stood in the hall and started to point his electronic measurer. I stepped into the bathroom to get out of the way. Behind him on the wall was a black and white photograph of my father, looking particularly handsome with his hair Brylcreamed into a wave. The agent didn't measure any other rooms but made his way into the kitchen. I offered him a straight-backed chair.

"Is this your chair?" he asked. "I don't need a cushion." I wasn't sure if he was being polite or fussy.

"I'm tall as well," was all I could think to say.

"We can arrange block viewings. We could get fifteen people at a time!" I imagined fifteen prospective buyers milling around the bungalow; fifteen people imagining themselves living in this home I'd been visiting for twenty-five years.

"What price are you after?"

"What would you say?"

"Two hundred and fifty."

"Would you go any higher?"

"No," he said abruptly. It was obvious there wasn't going to be any explanation to follow.

"What do you want the money for?"

"We're not sure really," I said, vaguely.

"Is that everything you want?" he asked.

When he got to the doorstep he turned to me.

"Do you have gas central heating?"

"Oil," I said.

"Is there gas up here?" I reassured him there was.

As he accelerated out of the drive the phone rang. It was Warren.

"How did it go?"

"We're not having him," I blurted out. "He can sod off! He wanted to know what we want the money for!"

"Why?!" said Warren.

"I don't know." I updated him with the conversations so far.

The third agent came the following afternoon. I had already received a letter to say that Marsha Wilcox would be arriving at 2.30pm and she would be very happy to talk to me about marketing opportunities. Marsha wore brown flowing trousers and a cropped jacket. She drove a contemporary jeep.

"Preston and Wilcox," she announced when I opened the door. She wanted to see the full extent of the property inside and out, including the garage.

"Lovely plot," she said. "Nice and private."

"You smell nice – what is it?" I asked as I lifted the garage door.

"Everyone says that. Calvin Klein Euphoria."

It wasn't until she was sitting on the sofa that Marsha really got started. She opened a company folder.

"Your information would go into all our four offices." She pointed at the photographs of their window displays on the back of the folder. "Our marketing is second to none. We're on all the national websites – which is where we get most of our interest. I'd advise you to keep some of the furniture and leave the carpets as they are – you won't gain anything by replacing them. I'd say two fifty."

"You wouldn't go any higher?"

"You could do 'offers over.' That way buyers would know you're serious about the two fifty. But any higher and people want a better kitchen and bathroom. When were you thinking of selling?"

"Well, it's my parents' home. They don't live here any more. My father died in January."

"I know what you're going through. My Mum died when I was twenty-two. I cried for three years. I still can't have a photograph of her anywhere near me."

"I'm sorry," I said.

"She was forty-six. Heart attack. I used to get out of bed and go down to the kitchen and cry into a tea towel – I didn't want my partner to see me. After three years I realized I was crying for myself, not for my Mum – you know – if I'd had a bad day."

"But you have to grieve," I said.

"If I had a good day I didn't cry for her. So I stopped. I know how hard it is."

"Would you put it on at two sixty?"

"If that's what you want. But really, people are going to come in here and say, out with the fireplace and out with the conservatory."

"I've never really liked that conservatory. But my parents did." They would entertain in there with the Royal Albert tea service and a plate of egg custard tarts. Even when Dad was quite ill, he laid new tiles on the floor.

"It really wants pulling down and building again. Even if you tidied up the garden – really cut it back…"

"Believe it or not we've spent quite a lot on the garden." Mum wasn't a tidy gardener. She preferred the privacy of tall trees. She hung baubles on an evergreen shrub at Christmas, and each night she brought in her two white plaster doves to shelter in the porch.

"We don't do block viewings." Marsha looked disgusted at the thought. "We attend every viewing personally. When you're ready get in touch."

We shook hands on the doorstep.

Later that afternoon I phoned my brother.

"We have to be sure this is what we want to do," I said. "Once it's sold we can't buy it back."

"I thought you needed the money."

"I thought *you* needed the money."

"Not really. I'm happy enough where I am."

"Well we can do without an extension."

"I just like being here," I said, knowing now that this was what I wanted. "I brought in the washing this morning and I remembered asking Mum if she wanted anything from the shops and she said, 'Get me a bottle of milk and a thong."

"I know," said Warren, laughing. "Shall we keep it then? See how we feel next spring?"

"Yes, let's do that."

I phoned the flooring men who had fitted the bathroom and kitchen vinyl the morning my father had died. We had talked about the possibility of carpets. I would get them done. We could enjoy the feel of them beneath our feet for a whole year.

20 Who Do You Thank for Your Gifts?

I'd have given anything to sleep a whole night through. Celia came recommended by a friend. I drove the length of her street in Hither Green, making sure of the house number then parked a few doors down. I wanted to approach the house from a distance. There were bits of old carpet on the path leading up to the front door. The sign on the wall had rusted; I could just make out the word 'Naturopath.'

The door opened. Celia, an elderly woman with a folded face stood unsmiling. I followed her as she limped in front of me. The house smelled of stewed tea and ancient tobacco. As I passed the back room I glimpsed an elderly man watching two different televisions at once – one football, one cooking.

At the top of the stairs Celia showed me into a small room. The massage table was just behind the door. The wall to the right was piled to the ceiling with old televisions, computers, and sagging black bags splitting with clothes and curtains. Beyond the massage table was a metal hospital screen rouched with off-white pleats; it was meant to hide larger discarded items – a bicycle without wheels, three rolls of carpet, and a crib. The curtains were half closed.

"Did your mother come here?" asked Celia. My mother had never moved out of a ten-mile radius of where she was born in Lancashire, so it seemed a random question.

"No."

I realized she was trying to place me.

"I heard about you through a friend – Michael Burn."

"Oh yes, Michael. Nice man."

Celia took a clipboard from the top of a pile of newspapers and produced a pen from her pocket.

"Give me your name and address."

I said the words slowly, spelling as I went along.

"Phone number?" She wrote down the information at the top of a blank piece of yellow paper.

"Oh, and the name of your doctor."

This was the extent of her note taking. She replaced the clipboard on the newspaper pile.

"Why have you come here?"

I tried to explain about not sleeping, and about my godmother who was dying. I felt like an open wound.

"Get undressed. Down to your bra and pants. I'll be just outside."

As she closed the door I noticed a light bulb at the end of a long piece of flex hanging on the back of the door. It was switched on.

"Are you ready?" she asked, before I was.

Part of me wanted to run out of the front door. If I'd been in my right mind I would have. But Celia might have the answer to my wakefulness; she might be able to relax me just enough to get me beyond those four medicated hours.

She began by patting parts of my body simultaneously – my forearms, the inside of my elbows, my knees, my calves. And then she smoothed my belly.

"Your tum tum," she said. "Everything that's ever happened to you is in there. You grew in your mummy's tummy. You were joined to her with an umbilical cord."

She rubbed her hands in oil and pummelled my thighs.

"You won't get all this with other people," she said as she pressed her fingers into my arms. "They just rub your body."

"Why won't you let her go – your godmother?"

I didn't know how to answer. How do you know that you need to let someone go?

"Do you go to church?"

"I don't believe in God."

"Why don't you believe? Did someone say something?"

I shook my head.

"Who do you thank for your gifts?" Again I didn't have an answer.

"Has anyone ever hurt you?"

"No," I said, knowing this was a ludicrous answer.

"There are four hurts in this world – injustice, humiliation, abandonment and betrayal. I had one client – her father had another woman so she refused to go to his funeral. She had a very bad pain in her arm. 'Cut off your arm,' I said. Then she forgave him, and the pain went away."

She pressed her fingers into my kneecap.

"You've injured your knee."

"Yes."

"Bursitis. Bursitis – inflammation of the bursa." She said this automatically, as though she had learned it by rote. "I'm a retired osteopath. I do that as well. I call it holistic." She explored my other knee without comment.

"Give me your thumbs. I won't take them far." She jogged them up and down.

"So you keep yourself pretty fit?"

"I walk a lot."

"You're putting your weight badly," she said, feeling the hard skin on my feet.

"Have you got a boyfriend?"

"Not any more."

"There's plenty more out there for you." She rubbed more oil onto her hands.

"Why did you break up with him?"

"He lived in another country."

"Do you have your parents?"

"No. Neither of them."

"Oh dear. When did they die?"

I mumbled an answer and then she was quiet for a while.

"Turn over."

My body was starting to feel warm and cared for, but I was now sure that I should have fled from this house at the first opportunity.

"Do you drink?"

"Very little."

"Any trouble with constipation?"

"No."

Again, she was silent for a while.

"Holidays?" I guessed she was asking if I had any plans.

"Haven't decided." I was in no position to make a decision about anything. Deciding what to eat was taxing enough.

She pressed the heels of her hands into my shoulders. Then she was silent for a long time. I much preferred it. My life felt like an amorphous mess which didn't bear much questioning. I tried to separate the comfort Celia was giving my body from the discomfort she was giving my mind with her constant interrogation.

Then out of nowhere she said, "We're going digital so now all the televisions won't work." Her statement hung in the air, unable to connect with any of the previous conversations.

The hour came to an end. I pushed myself up with my arms, swung my legs over the side of the table and reached for my clothes.

"That's right, you get dressed now." Celia didn't leave the room as I would have expected. She sat on the edge of the massage table and looked into space. When I was dressed I put three ten pound notes into her hand.

"Do your best for your godmother," she said. "Pray to God if it gets bad, even if you don't believe. He'll help you."

Again I woke that night after four hours' sleep. I lay alert and inert till the morning light.

21 Daughter, God-daughter

Husk

I pulled up in the car park in front of Springbank House nursing home. Sunday was *the* day for visiting. All the cars, marshalled into neat rows, were bigger than mine. It was a sacred Sunday in December; the sky was clear, the light as strong and penetrating as it could be so near to the solstice.

Alice and I looked at one another. Alice's complexion was always pale, but now her skin was like milk which had lost its cream.

"Can I give you some cake?" said Alice.

"Yes, please." She handed me a portion of poppy seed cake wrapped in foil, sent down by her sister from Leeds.

"I don't know how long I'll be," Alice said.

"Don't worry. Be as long as you like."

"How about if I meet you here at three, and let you know how it's going?" It was one o'clock by then.

"That's fine," I said.

"Do you want to come in and I'll show you where you can make a cup of tea?"

"That would be good. I'm desperate for the loo as well."

"Sure. And I'll tell the staff who you are." I nodded.

"Thanks for doing this," said Alice. The trains were erratic that day, and she very much wanted to visit her mother again before beginning another working week. Her visit earlier in the week had been distressing – both for her and her mother. Alice wanted a different atmosphere to lie over the room where her mother lay on a rippling mattress, surrounded by spindle berries from her cherished garden. So I'd picked Alice up at Clapham South and we'd driven down to Esher.

I'd known Alice's mother, Merryn, for almost as long as I'd known Alice. Twenty-five years. Alice and I met on our first day at art college. Alice had a flask of coffee and I had a stack of sandwiches; we pooled our resources. At first I visited Alice's parents *with* Alice; then, after Merryn's husband died, I visited on my own.

We'd have lunch, weed and lop together, then drop accumulated cuttings off at the council tip. We'd have tea in the living room, with extra hot water on standby from the kettle beside Merryn's winged armchair. There'd be extended conversations over iced coffee biscuits, fruitcake and shortbread. There was a day in March we went on an outing. We had Wisley gardens almost to ourselves. Merryn scrambled through the mud and rain to scrutinize any plant which caught her eye. We both stood mesmerized by a bank dotted with yellow hoop petticoat narcissus. When a rat moved into my flat and ate my soap, Merryn sent a selection of fragrant new soaps. When my car crashed, she sent Garrison Keillor.

"I feel embarrassed that you're not going to see her," said Alice as we approached the A3. Now that Merryn was dying she wanted only closest family to visit.

"That's alright. I wouldn't want it any other way." I was glad to be able to help. Since Alice had told me of Merryn's brain tumour three months before, I had slipped into a treacly chasm.

The nursing home was a triple fronted substantial Victorian house, with just enough charm to make it attractive. There was a hanging basket beside the front door. Alice peered into it. "The pansies have revived. They were limp when I came on Tuesday. Frosted."

Alice remembered the code to open the front door and whispered it in my ear. The warmth of the house was welcome, but not oppressive. There was a display of silk flowers on the hall table, and a notice board with photographs of residents blowing out birthday candles and opening presents. The Christmas decorations were thankfully minimal and subtle.

Alice showed me the kitchen, the kettle, the cupboard with mugs, and the jars of instant coffee and dusty teabags. As we climbed the stairs I noticed the framed prints staggered up the wall – wheelbarrows, ancient farm equipment, botanical illustrations. Alice pointed to the toilet at the end of the landing.

"Just tell me where your Mum is," I asked. I knew she was near, and needed to place her in this warren of doors and corridors.

"She's at the end of that landing, on the left." Alice pointed in the opposite direction, then kissed me on both cheeks. She managed a smile as she walked away.

Every door carried the name of the person inside. 'Doris Precious' was behind the door next to the toilet. On each door handle hung a hand-stitched toy – a long limbed monkey, a ballerina, a billowing clown. I wasn't sure if they were part of the Christmas decorations or permanent fixtures. Were they supposed to remind the staff before they entered the room that each resident had once been a child? Were they there to help the residents feel they were individuals, and not merely part of an institution?

I knew something of what was inside Merryn's room from what Alice had told me. Above her bed was the shield of Cornwall, her home county – a triangle of golden coins on a black background. Beside her bed were three books – 'Alice in Wonderland' with Tenniel's drawings, 'A Midsummer Night's Dream' and 'The Merchant of Venice'. Merryn had asked Alice to read to her from 'Alice in Wonderland' – from the chapter which begins with the playing-card-gardeners painting a white rose tree red. There was also a pinboard displaying all the cards she had received, including the ones from me – a Zuberon still life with cup and rose, a serene Morandi, an early jewelled Rothko, and Leonardo's pencil studies of violets and cherry blossom. Merryn, who had lived all her life without a television, now requested DVD's – 'Blithe Spirit' and 'The Hound of the Baskervilles'. And finally, 'Henry V'. At first Merryn replied to my cards, her always-welcome handwriting only a little shaky. On the first envelope she remembered all of my address apart from the house number. On the second there were three kisses by my name, and the address had been added by someone else. The final two envelopes were addressed by Alice.

I struggled to know what to say when I wrote the cards. At first I caught her up with my projects, reported back on the nasturtiums and nicotania sylvestris still flowering in my garden. But as I inched slowly towards accepting that Merryn was going to die, I realized I had to say what was in my heart.

'You've always been such a lovely friend, darling,' said Merryn in her first card – the Cutty Sark racing home for the Royal National Lifeboat Institution. She had written 'Ship Ahoy!' beside her greeting. In her second her mind must have been ranging over her life; she'd been thinking of the Gregorian chant books she'd seen in Italy with her husband, and of large floppy butterflies being poked by birds. She'd ordered bulbs for a special 'Spring Display' at her home she'd left in Esher. Her third card commented on my Leonardo card – how he must have drawn the violets and cherry blossom straight away, as they were so obviously fresh.

In Merryn's final card, Alice now her amanuensis, she said how much she appreciated the cards, but really I mustn't feel the need to send many more because she knew how much I had to do, and the important thing was that I had time for my writing and painting. I took this last consideration as rejection. My skin was so thin at that time it couldn't protect me, not even from the glance of a feather.

I let myself out of Springbank House, the door clicking behind me. Alice had pointed out a side road which led to a path across some fields. The gardens of the compact cottages along the road were straddled with the skeletons of summer – hollyhock stalks with bulging seed heads, the blots of rudbekias, plates of sedums and alchemilla. The path rose up and over a bridge then ran alongside a field of caramel cows. I could see puddles in the depressions in the path, sealed with thin sheets of ice. When I gently pressed my foot on the ice lids, bubbles jostled beneath the surface.

I thought about the house that Merryn had left behind; the sight of the 1930's gable which heralded every visit, mauve candy tuft by the front door, pink amaryllis strengthening under the bay, a jasmine hedge to inhale on arrival. My eyes would rove as I made for the front door's throaty bell and Merryn's warm welcome; purple morning glory climbing the fence, the leaves of cyclamen nestling in the beds, a lavender bush making its presence felt beside the path. How must it have been for her to think of leaving all this behind? The carved oak writing desk in the front room where she pursued her correspondence with bishops and prime ministers; the dining table in the back room where so many celebratory meals had been eaten with family and friends; the glass-covered bookshelves in both rooms holding Milton, Donne, Clare, Marvell.

Alice said that since being admitted to Springbank House Merryn hadn't mentioned her home, apart from indicating precisely where in the back garden the bulbs she had ordered should be planted. This made Alice think that managing it had become too much for her. But at some point, at many points, Merryn must have thought about how it would be to leave her home.

A cyclist came up behind me, rode through a collection of puddles and crunched the ice into jagged pieces. The lemon light was low and the sun no longer visible. I turned back and retraced my steps.

In the car I listened to the radio and ate the poppy seed cake. By three o'clock every window was steamed up. I saw Alice appear at the front door, she scanned the car park for my silver-blue Peugeot. I switched on the windscreen wipers and waved out of the window. Alice waved back, ran over, and eased herself into the passenger seat.

"I couldn't find you. I thought your car was red. So much for visual acuity."

"Almost right. My last car was red. How is she?"

Alice sighed. "She's like a husk."

"Oh, love."

"She says she's content. She can't say she's happy, but she's content."

"Could she chat?"

"She told me she loves me."

Indian Soap

I parked my car on a side street off the South Circular and slammed the door particularly hard. I resented having to come here every Wednesday night for eight o'clock. Though it *was* my choice. Or was it? I didn't see myself as having a choice. Before the first appointment I'd been so apprehensive I had to tackle my geraniums to keep control of myself. I took them down from their shelf – pink, pinker, white and pink – and one by one stripped them of their dead leaves.

It was a dark dank night; not cold enough to be invigorating, and not warm enough to dry the pavements of rain. I pressed the bell of the Garret Centre. The timing had to be exactly right. The therapists had to have ended their previous session in order to be able to answer the door. It might be my own therapist who answered, more often than not it wasn't.

I sat in the waiting room, waiting to be called. The occupants barely acknowledged each other, despite their proximity. I watched the minutes tick away, wondering what we would talk about. At this stage it never seemed to me that there was anything *to* talk about.

Sylvia appeared. I followed her up the stairs. I resented Sylvia's black leather boots, her silk pleated skirt, her glossy blonde hair. I couldn't remember when I'd last taken an interest in my appearance – I picked up the same clothes day after day.

Sylvia was slight and graceful, I felt heavy and leaden. I walked through the door of her room, took off my coat and sat in the chair next to the window and the radiator. The thin navy curtains were not quite closed, but I could see the streetlights through the gap. I wouldn't look out of the window again till the end of the session.

Sylvia always waited for me to speak first.

"Merryn died at the weekend."

"How did you find out?"

"Alice phoned me." I paused. "But I think I already knew. Merryn sent me some soap. A selection. There was an emerald green one, from India. Aromatic. Wonderful. On Saturday I cleaned the bathroom – there were just two small pieces left on the sink. When I looked again the pieces had formed themselves into a heart shape." I paused again. "I didn't get upset. My heart was heavy. But I think I've grieved already."

"You'd been doing a lot of grieving. And it must be very difficult for you because you're a friend of the family, not a family member. You must feel as though you are very much on the outside."

I didn't feel this, and I was surprised by what she said, but I didn't contradict her.

"Alice has asked me to read 'The Wren' by John Clare at the funeral."

A double decker bus accelerated on the road outside.

"I stopped sleeping when Merryn was first diagnosed. I was asked by two different doctors within forty-eight hours if I intended to take my own life."

"That must have been frightening."

"I was already frightened… I don't understand why I can't sleep."

"Are you still taking medication?"

"Sleeping tablets and anti-depressants. The sleeping tablets give me four hours a night then I wake up."

"The feelings you are having are too painful to allow you to sleep." This sounded too glib an explanation to me, but I did like its simplicity. I looked at the clock which stood on a filing cabinet to the left of Sylvia. Sylvia glanced at the clock above my head.

"Do you think I should do my school bookings next week?"

"How many days is it?"

"Three. Two nights away from home. In Cumbria."

"I think it's time to re-connect with that part of yourself. Your career is very important to you."

"The alternative is very bleak. To not do them. But everything feels such hard work."

There was a pause.

"A friend phoned me yesterday morning. I was concentrating on just trying to feel normal. I only told her last week how I am. She knows about my Mum – her manic depression, or bi-polar or whatever you call it… It took me a long time to tell her."

"Because of the shame you felt?" Sylvie crossed her legs.

"I suppose so."

"She said, 'Did your father suffer from depression?' She's driving along in her car and she asks me a question like that! It knocked me right back. I'm trying to talk about what's happening to me so people get an idea of what it's like. But saying something like that – she's *no* idea. *And* she's suffered from depression herself!"

There was another pause. Sylvie held my gaze.

"Another friend suggested I become a volunteer at the Dulwich Picture Gallery. I can't volunteer in my own life, let alone the Dulwich Picture Gallery. People don't know what you need. Most people."

"What do you need?"

"For people just to be there. To listen. Not to leave me alone."

"It's good that you are trying to explain. And I have to say you are working very hard in these sessions, and between the sessions."

I looked at the spider plants cascading down the table behind Sylvia.

"When Merryn adopted me as her god-daughter at her husband's funeral she asked me to go down and help her with the garden. We'd talk and talk and talk. She was interested in everything."

"I think one of the reasons you have felt the loss so deeply is that you could be a child with Merryn. You talk about chatting and having tea... You didn't have any responsibility for her. These are very old feelings we are dealing with. You couldn't be a child with your own mother – you had too much responsibility."

"It wasn't her fault," I said fiercely.

Lemon Chiffon

As we left the house to attend the funeral Alice said goodbye to her mother once more. Goodbye to her bent fingers which arranged gentians and sweet peas in delicate vases for the dining table, goodbye to her soft cheek which she pressed against Alice's in greeting, goodbye to her trickling voice which stroked Alice's's wounds and sang at her every triumph.

"Are you alright carrying that?" I asked Alice as we went out of the front door. I had driven down from London to Esher with two massive lemon chiffon cakes which Alice had ordered the week before. 'Three layers of citrus sponge filled and iced with tangy lemon frosting, made with organic unwaxed lemons. The perfect celebration cake,' said the Konditor and Cook website.

"I'm fine. How about you, Kitty?" asked Alice looking behind her. Kitty was Alice's older sister. She was clasping the other cake close to her chest.

"It is heavy but I'm sure I'll manage," said Kitty.

"We can take it in turns," I said.

"I've got two strong arms," said Rosemary, clenching her fists.

It was three years since I had buried my own mother. I'd kept all her silver toast racks. In my studio in New Cross

I was making pencil drawings of each one. The walls were lined with evocations – shiny ribbed bars welded to looped handles.

The four of us assembled on the pavement.

"How long will it take to get to the church hall?" I asked.

"About twenty minutes," said Alice.

"I just needed to know."

"Of course."

Alice looked back at the house. The winter flowering jasmine was shooting its yellow flowers around the front door, two stone pots stood on either side smug with the promise of Queen of the Night tulips. I went to stand beside Alice. She leaned her head on my shoulder until she was ready to go.

We wound around the suburban streets, passing ample semis with mature gardens. As we approached the traffic lights on the main road Alice rested her cake on a garden wall.

"Shall I take over?" I asked.

"Yes, please," said Alice. "I don't think I've got much upper arm strength."

"I'm not sure I've got much more," I said.

"Can I take yours?" said Rosemary to Kitty.

"I'd like that. Shall I carry your bag?" Kitty placed the white box on Rosemary's outstretched arms; Rosemary wrapped her gloved hands around it.

"How are Peter and Sarah?" I asked Kitty.

"Oh, they're fine. Peter will probably be knocking seven bells out of a football, and Sarah... putting whale stickers on her exercise books. Something like that."

Kitty lived two hundred miles from her mother's house. In recent months when she was looking after her children she thought she should be looking after her mother. When she was looking after her mother she thought she should be with her children. Her mother's death had ended that particular dilemma. But now, when she was back in Leeds, she inhabited every room of her mother's house. She saw Merryn sifting her fingers through the buds of lavender which she'd rubbed into Chinese porcelain bowls. She heard the rattling of silver cutlery as Merryn replaced it in the felt-lined drawer. She saw her gazing at the arching leaves of five amaryllis stored in the back bedroom as they waited to bloom downstairs.

"Not far to go now," said Alice encouragingly as we rounded the last corner.

Rosemary lived five thousand miles from *her* mother. She'd left her behind in Zimbabwe. They spoke on the phone occasionally and Rosemary sent her money regularly. Merryn had greeted Rosemary when she first saw her, as she did everyone she met in her road. Rosemary asked if she knew anyone who needed a cleaner. Merryn had been meaning to get help, so Rosemary began to clean for her. As Merryn became more frail she took increasing care of her. They both said an angel had brought them together.

By the time we arrived at the church hall we'd all carried each cake once. The verdict was that one cake was heavier than the other. We dropped them off at the village hall and made our way to the church opposite. Alice pointed out the English flag flying over the church steeple at half-mast. Not many parishioners were given this honour. The verger met us at the doorway wearing a red fleece. "I must apologize," she said, "I'm not properly dressed yet. It's just so cold." The church was already filling up.

The vicar told of Merryn, and Peter – the man she had married. How he was a friend of her brother's at Cambridge, and due to visit their Cornish home during the summer holidays for the second year running. Merryn mounted her bicycle and pedalled into St Austell. She came back carrying three new dresses. "I had nothing to wear," she told her family. They realized then there was something brewing. Within six months Peter and Merryn were married.

When the service was over the seventy or so congregation funnelled into the church hall. Vases of early narcissus and sprays of leaves from Merryn's garden had been placed at intervals around the windowsills and on the stage. A table held a selection of colour and black and white photographs of Merryn, from when she was a toddler, to a sunny lunch on a recent holiday in Greece. The two yellow moon-cakes stood on a table opposite, at the end of lines of teacups and sherry glasses. The words on the top of each cake – 'Merryn, with love' – were piped in red icing between hearts and stars.

Kitty and Alice went from group to group thanking their friends and relatives for coming. A man approached them for details of their family, so that he could make a page on the church website about the funeral. A woman approached Alice to ask for Rosemary's details, so that she could offer her some cleaning work. Rosemary and I sat together at a table near the cakes with a plate of food each from the buffet.

"I'm going to measure those cakes and see if one *is* bigger than the other," I said.

I used my fork to measure their diameters, flipping it over till I reached the far side of each cake.

"I'm right. This one is nearly a third of a fork bigger!"

Rosemary laughed and I sat down again.

"How do you find living in Esher?" I asked.

"Some people are nice, some aren't. Last week I got told to go back to Brixton."

"Oh dear."

"My local church isn't very friendly. I go to Croydon to pray."

"That's rather a long way."

"I came here to live with my sister. She's a nurse. But she moved to America."

Just then the caterer thought she should cut the cakes and have them ready for anyone who wanted to eat something sweet. She took a large knife from the kitchen and began to slice the first cake. I scraped back my chair and darted over to Alice.

"Letting you know that the cakes are now being cut. Not sure if that's what you wanted," I said quietly.

"Thank you," said Alice. She got to the cake table as the second slice was being cut.

"Do you mind if *I* cut the cakes?" she asked.

"No, not at all." The caterer handed her the knife.

Alice pointed the knife into the centre of the cake and felt the resistance of the dense sponge as she pressed gently downwards. She tipped the slice over onto its side and slid the knife underneath before slithering it onto a waiting plate. The guests began to gather round. Alice sliced the rest of the cake and handed out each plate with a smile and a serviette. Then she set about the second cake.

The may was out in June. Along the drenched M62 bushes clung to the sides of the hills spattering white across their contours. Trenches of cow parsley lined the top road down into Ramsbottom. As I turned into the drive I could see that the bungalow's 'For Sale' sign was now a 'Sold' sign. The lawns were meadows. I waited for three mallards to waddle away from the driveway before I could park.

On the Saturday I did much as I usually did – went to the market, bought bird seed, peanuts, tasty Lancashire cheese; looked at the plant stall and appreciated the hills to the east and the west. There was a huge salmon on the fish stall with a sign written in royal blue marker pen – 'I'm the Daddy'.

"Can I take a photo?" I asked the owner.

"You're not from the Inland Revenue are you?" he asked. His ruddy cheeks were curved around a smile.

I walked around the end of the stall to line up the fish and the sign.

"I'm going to put this on facebook," I said.

"Tell them my name is Mr Patel and I don't come from this country," said the owner.

On Bridge Street a woman passed me wearing a mink stole complete with head and feet, a felt hat and high heels. She was followed by a man in a US Air Force uniform. The war had come to Ramsbottom.

In the newsagents I asked where the 1940's weekend was based.

"They're all going to the railway station," said the shop assistant. "We had a tank drive through the village last year."

"Yes, they parachuted it in, just like they did in the war!" said her husband. "And did the yanks come to Ramsbottom?

I don't think so!"

"We had a nazi came in one year for a quarter of barley sugars," said his wife.

I made a glottal gasp, took my change and left.

Great globes of mauve rhododendrons were flowering on the approach to the bungalow. A few had survived in our garden at the boundary with the neighbours.

I could still sit on Mum's Lloyd Loom skirted armchair and read the paper, drink tea from the cricket table, watch the bullfinches pecking at the neighbour's squirrel-proof feeder, watch the squirrels feeding too. But when Warren arrived the next day he went through the bungalow like a tornado. There were bags for the tip, boxes for the charity shop and baskets of cutlery and crockery to take home. There were paint tins to choose from, garden tools and sets of saucepans. If the heavy green hoover went to the tip how would I hoover before I left? Would the new people want a supply of old newspapers? Would they appreciate a milk jug, a red plastic sieve, a lawnmower?

By the time Warren left the only piece of furniture left standing was a single upright chair. I couldn't stay any longer. I would leave the next day.

The morning sun shone through the tips of the honeysuckle by the back door. I watched the copper beaches swaying in the wind. Then I walked from room to room. I remembered Christmas dinners and buffets in the dining room, parties in the sitting room, coming together in the kitchen. I noted who had slept in each bedroom. As I stood in Mum's bedroom I could see the white outline of a large bird on the window. It must have flown against the glass. Each wing feather of its wide span was imprinted like an intricate chalk dust drawing. After seeing this I could leave.

I drove the long way round to the motorway – over Owd Betts. The folding hills were emerald. I could see for miles. The horizon dissolved into sky.

Acknowledgments

My grateful thanks to the editors of the following publications where earlier versions of these stories first appeared: 'Between Here and Knitwear' in *Cadenza*, 'American Tan' in *How Maxine Learned to Love Her Legs* (Aurora Metro), 'Lady Macbeth' in *Northwords Now*, 'Stepping in the Dark' and 'Flowers of the Forest' in *The Family Connections* (Salt), 'Piercings' in *The Family section of The Guardian*, 'Paper' in *Ink Sweat and Tears*, 'Red Leatherette' in *The Lampeter Review*, 'Curlew' in *Wales Arts Review*, 'Daughter, God-daughter' in *Unthology 6* (Unthank Books). 'Between Here and Knitwear' was also read by the author on BBCR4's afternoon story slot.

'A Small Smudge of Blood' was one of six equal winners in the ICA New Blood short story competition judged by Alison Fell and Kevin Toolis. 'A Small Smudge of Blood' and 'Lady Macbeth' were highly commended by Ali Smith, William Fiennes and Edward Platt in the New Writing Ventures Awards.

My thanks also to the Oppenheim-John Downes Memorial Trust for an award which helped me to complete this collection. My thanks also to my friends who took time to read early manuscripts, to my family and friends for their unending support, and to Robin Jones for his perspicacity and patience.

Biography

Chrissie Gittins was born in Lancashire and lives in Forest Hill, London. Her first poetry collection is *Armature* (Arc, 2003) and her second is *I'll Dress One Night As You* (Salt, 2009). Her third poetry pamphlet is *Professor Heger's Daughter* (Paekakariki Press, 2013). Her stories and poems have been broadcast on BBCR4 and her four radio plays were all Radio Choices in the Radio Times and in various newspapers. Chrissie's first short story collection is *Family Connections* (Salt, 2007). She has written three poetry collections for children which have been named Choices for the Children's Poetry Bookshelf; *Now You See Me, Now You...* (Rabbit Hole, 2002) and *I Don't Want an Avocado for an Uncle* (Rabbit Hole, 2006) were also shortlisted for the CLPE Poetry Award. Her third children's collection is *The Humpback's Wail* (Rabbit Hole, 2010). In 2014 Bloomsbury published her new and collected children's poems *Stars in Jars*; in the same year Chrissie was a finalist in the first Manchester Children's Literature Prize with a portfolio of new poems. She has made an hour's recording of her children's poems for the Poetry Archive, and her poems have been animated for Cbeebies TV. She has read her work at many venues and festivals including Hay, Wigtown, Edinburgh, Stanza and The Poets House New York. Chrissie has received two Arts Council Writers' Awards, and awards from The Royal Literary Fund and the Author's Foundation. She is included in the British Council directory of UK and Commonwealth writers and is honorary Writer in Residence with Lewisham Borough.

www.chrissiegittins.co.uk